AUDREY'S AWAKENING

As always, this book is dedicated to my family. Every one of you have shown support and belief in me and it means more than you could know.

And, to my readers. Having fans who support my writing and who enjoy the stories I create, gives me the encouragement I need to keep writing. I can't thank you all enough.

CHAPTER 1

"C'mon darlin'...you look like you need a good strong man to take care of you." The man slurred his words, obviously having come straight from the tavern up the street.

Audrey kept walking, holding her head up and staring straight ahead down the main dirt road in Bethany. The man followed right behind her and she could smell the alcohol on his breath as he leaned in closer.

"Keep your hands off me." Her voice shook but she hoped the man didn't notice. She pulled her shawl up around her shoulders and tried to get her legs to move faster, heading for the boarding house where she was staying.

"Oh, c'mon. Just a lil' kiss..." The man's voice stopped suddenly and another voice broke in.

"The lady said to leave her alone, Harlan."

Audrey sighed with relief at the sound of Reid's voice.

Reid Wallace was well known in the Willamette Valley area, where the new settlement of Bethany was located. He was also the brother of the man who had just married her best friend. She'd met him a few times and was grateful to see the familiar face as she turned to him.

Harlan Baker, the drunk who'd been bothering her, was normally quite harmless, known to be a drinker by everyone in the settlement. He worked at the flour mill on the edge of town but spent a great deal of time "playing cards", as he put it, at the small tavern in town. Audrey had run into him a few times since arriving in Bethany and usually just tried to stay out of his way.

However, this time she'd been so lost in thought as she admired the beauty of the humble settlement nestled in among the trees, she didn't even notice him coming up beside her.

"Ah, Reid, I wasn't meanin' her no harm." The older man patted the younger one on the arm, giving him a toothless grin. "I was jus' gonna help her get home safely."

"I'll take it from here, Harlan. Thank you for your concern." Reid tipped his hat toward the man, then took Audrey's arm and led her away.

"Need to be careful when walking around on your own out here. Not many women around these parts, so a woman on her own can draw a lot of attention." Reid wasn't much for small talk.

"I know. I am normally much more careful. I guess I was just lost in my thoughts and wasn't paying much attention." She offered a smile as she stole a glance up at the man beside her.

She couldn't help but notice the tightness of his jaw and the way he never smiled. His jaw was covered with a slight brushing of stubble, hard to see under the shadow of the large hat he wore. She knew his eyes were a deep blue, the same color as everyone in his family. It was something she'd noticed about him when they first met.

"Well, Harlan is pretty harmless but you never know who else is roaming around. Bethany has all kinds of drifters moving through on their way down to California or coming in from back east on the wagon trains."

Feeling much like a chastised child, she couldn't help but feel a bit embarrassed. She stopped to turn and face him, then waited until he stopped and glanced back at her.

"I appreciate your concern, Reid; however, I am able to take care of myself. I made it all this way from Missouri on my own and I am quite certain I can handle the town drunk." She felt bad as she gazed into the eyes staring back at her. She knew he was only trying to help.

"But thank you for helping me. And, I will be

more careful in the future." She smiled warmly at him, wishing she could see what he looked like when *he* smiled.

She wasn't going to see it today, though. After standing and staring at her for what seemed like a lifetime, he simply nodded his head and turned to go back the direction they had just come from. She hadn't even noticed they were standing in front of the boarding house.

Her eyes followed the man walking away from her. He was so different from the man she'd traveled from Missouri with—her husband, Pete. She and Pete had only been married for a few short weeks when cholera took him from her on the wagon train headed to Oregon.

Her heart wrenched as she thought of her late husband, such a contrast from the man who'd just walked away from her. Where Pete was friendly, outgoing, and happy, Reid was quiet and kept to himself. And, he carried sadness around him like a cloak.

Pete had been her sweetheart for as long as she could remember. They always knew they would marry but after her father announced he'd arranged for her to marry a man back home in Kentucky, they were forced to elope.

Then, when Pete died on the trail west, she was left alone, unable to turn around and go home but unsure what the future would hold for her once she made it to Oregon. She made the decision to finish the journey and follow through on her and Pete's dream of building a life out here.

Feeling wetness building in her eyes as the memories flooded in, she swallowed hard and blinked the tears away. She glanced up to see that Reid was back at the blacksmiths', where he'd left his horse, and he was talking with the man there. Then he turned to walk across the street to the feed store.

If she weren't still so in love with Pete, she could almost think she was feeling something stirring in her as she watched the other man.

He glanced up and caught her standing, staring at him. Her cheeks burned in embarrassment. Quickly turning, she raced up the steps and ran inside, almost knocking over Dorothy Larsen, the kind older woman who managed the boarding house.

"My dear, you look like you're running from the devil himself!" The plump woman threw her hand to her chest while reaching out with the other to grab the stair railing and keep herself from toppling over.

"I'm so sorry, Mrs. Larsen! I don't know what's wrong with me today! I seem to be so muddle-headed." She offered the woman a smile and put her hand out to steady her.

"I'm just going to head up to my room to change

and I will be right back down to help get dinner ready for the guests." She'd been helping Mrs. Larsen with the cooking and cleaning around there since she arrived. Her work was helping to pay her way. Because the woman had just lost her helper right before Audrey showed up seeking work, the older woman appreciated the fact that Audrey loved to cook and bake.

Opening the door to her room, she walked over to the edge of the bed and sat. She stared at the small jewelry box her husband had made her before they left home and let the tears that had been building fall. Guilt for how she felt when staring at Reid tore at her heart which combined with the grief she still carried over losing Pete. The tears fell faster.

She laid back on the bed and let the tears flow. The worries that had burdened her since arriving in Bethany overwhelmed her and the stirrings she'd felt when with Reid just seemed to be the straw that broke the donkey's back.

How could she think of any other man, especially so soon after losing her own husband, a man who had loved her beyond reason? She knew it was just loneliness but it didn't make it any easier.

It wasn't fair. All of their dreams and hopes were gone. And now, she was lying here alone, unsure of what her future held. She had to decide, by spring, what she was going to do. If she went home, she knew she'd have to follow through with her father's plans and marry Frank Hillman.

Frank was quite high on Lexington's society ladder, making him much sought after in social circles. All of Audrey's acquaintances were so jealous of her betrothal to him.

It didn't matter that she didn't want to marry him. No one cared that her heart belonged to another. Her father had a reputation to uphold and debts to repay, so marrying into the Hillmans would give him everything he needed.

And now, she'd thrown all of that away to run off with Pete. She didn't know if she would be welcomed back home or if she even wanted to try. Her heart already belonged in Oregon, where she had dreamed of settling far away from the status-seeking society people who had never made her feel like she belonged.

She sat up and dried her eyes on her sleeve, then stood to walk to the dresser. She picked up the tiny box, held it in her hands, squeezed her eyes shut, and prayed for Pete to send her some sign to let her know what to do.

In the silence, a breeze blew into the room through the open window and she could hear the sound of horse's hooves trotting past. She opened her eyes, looked out the window, and saw Reid Wallace riding out of town.

She wasn't sure why but a calmness enveloped

her and she sensed it was somehow related to the man she was once again watching.

Audrey shook her head and took a deep breath. Whatever was going to happen would be decided soon. A letter had already been sent to her family, letting them know of Pete's death, so she had no doubt she'd learn of her fate soon.

She just hoped that this time, she might have some say in the matter.

CHAPTER 2

"So what will you do now that Ella is working out on Walter Jenkins' ranch?" Colton leaned back in the chair on Reid's front porch where they were watching Reid's daughter, Sophia, giggling and trying to catch up to the woman coaxing her to walk on her own. "And, now that my house is almost finished, Phoebe and I won't be staying here much longer. You won't have her to help with Sophia, either. You'll need to decide what you're going to do. You can't care for a baby and plant your crops in the spring—unless you plan to strap her to your back as you run the plow through the dirt."

Reid sighed and ran his hand through his hair, staring thoughtfully down at his worn boots. He was tired and he didn't want to talk about his plans for the future. At this moment, he didn't even know the plans himself.

His younger brother Colton had married Phoebe soon after arriving in Oregon a few weeks ago and they had been staying with him while the family helped build them their own house on the edge of the property.

His house was small, so he had moved to a room in the barn so the newlyweds could have his room. Colton's wife, Phoebe, had a younger sister, Grace, who shared the loft with Sophia while they were there. Both ladies were a huge help with the baby.

But, Colton was right. They wouldn't be staying there much longer and now that his sister Ella was working out at the neighboring ranch, there'd be no one to help him. He couldn't keep asking his mother to help, even though he knew she would never refuse.

The breeze that kissed his face was cool, reminding him that winter was approaching. A sound brought his gaze up to the road leading to the homestead and he saw the family wagon approaching. His mother, sister Ella, and brothers, Logan and Connor, were inside. They'd been in town for church that morning and today was his turn to host the family picnic.

For as long as he could remember, each Sunday after church, his family would spend the day together. They'd done it before they came west and the tradition continued even after they arrived in Oregon.

Sometimes, others from the town would come out and join them. Because today was still warm and beautiful, he knew a few others from town would trickle by to enjoy the company together outdoors.

He stood to go help his mother and sister out of the wagon and saw another wagon approaching around the bend toward the house. He raised his hand to shield his eyes and noticed Susan and James O'Hara, the kind older couple who'd ridden the wagon train with Colton and Phoebe. They had taken over the mercantile in town and became fast friends with everyone in the small community.

The woman who ran the boarding house, Dorothy Larsen, was sitting in the back of their wagon but his eyes were drawn to the petite figure sitting beside her. He recognized Audrey Thomsen immediately and his heart gave a strange flutter when she turned and smiled at him. She lifted her arm to wave so he nodded his head and then turned back to help his mother from her wagon.

"You could try to take the scowl off your face for one day, Reid." His mother pinned him with her gaze as he reached up to grab her waist and lift her down. Reid heard Ella scream as Colton reached up and dragged her from the wagon. They were twins and they seemed to go out of their way to annoy each other.

He offered his mother a weak attempt at a smile so she wouldn't keep bothering him and then he tipped his hat and walked back to help the ladies out of the other wagon.

Susan O'Hara smiled down at him from the wagon seat and then again when she was safely on the ground. "Oh, thank you, Reid! Isn't it just a beautiful day? Thank you for inviting us out to spend the day with your family. My James and I miss our own families back East, so days we can spend with friends are always cherished." Susan O'Hara was a kind woman who thought it was important to thank him even though it was his mother who had invited everyone out for the day.

"No trouble at all, Mrs. O'Hara. You are always welcome." He turned back to the wagon to help Dorothy down but was shocked into immobility at Audrey's bright smile. He glanced to the other side of the wagon and saw Colton grinning at him like a fool as he stepped up to help Dorothy down.

"Yes, Reid, thank you for including us today. The days can be long and lonely, so spending time with your family always puts a smile on my face." She held her hand out to him.

He took her hand then let her put her foot onto the small step on the side. She tried to step down but her dress caught under her shoe. She fell forward and, before he knew what happened, she was in his arms. Her face was inches from his and the slight scent of lilac teased his nose.

He couldn't help but notice how light she felt in

his arms or the shine of her dark hair that was peeking out beneath her bonnet.

"Oh my! I'm so sorry, Reid! Thank you for catching me." Her voice trembled as she gazed up at him with embarrassment in her eyes.

All he could do was nod. "You need to be more careful." With those words, he set her away from him and turned to walk over to where the others were gathering in front of the house.

The women were already pulling picnic baskets from the wagons and Phoebe emerged from the house with her arms full of even more delectable offerings. He watched Colton race to help her and his heart wrenched at the love he saw between them.

He had felt that love before. Once. But now there was just an empty space in his heart where those feelings had lived. No matter how hard he tried to erase the pain, it only got worse.

He shook his head, determined to enjoy the day, and followed the others to the back of the house. There was a quiet cluster of trees along the creek where he'd often come to sit and clear his thoughts. He tried not to let his eyes move to the spot where he'd spent time sitting with Eliza, dreaming of their future with the baby they were expecting.

Once the food was all set out, everyone filled their plates. He let his mother help Sophia as he took his own plate and sat off to the side. He loved his family, but sometimes they were too much for even him.

His youngest brother, Connor, came and sat beside him, folding his long legs and sitting in the dirt beside his big brother. Even though he was only seventeen, he already stood taller than most men.

"Mind if I hide over here with you?" Reid smiled at him.

"Grace can still find you over here, you know."

Everyone noticed how Phoebe's younger sister had taken a liking to Connor. Grace followed him relentlessly and Connor didn't have the patience for a girl he said was too young for him. But, it didn't stop her from trying.

Reid and Connor ate in silence for a few minutes, listening to the voices and the laughter filling the air around them.

"Audrey Thomsen seems nice." Reid sputtered as he choked on the biscuit he'd just bit down on. He glared over at Connor who was glancing toward the woman he mentioned as though he hadn't just said anything out of the ordinary at all.

Reid sat staring at his brother, waiting for him to turn and face him. "Yes, I'm sure she is lovely. What are you getting at?" He wasn't in the mood for small talk about a woman. And, if Connor thought he had any chance with an older woman, Reid was afraid he would be in for some heartbreak.

Connor chuckled to himself as he took a bite from his piece of pie. "Nothin'. Just stating a fact."

"Well, if you've got any notions about chasing after a woman who is at least three years older than you, and who has already been married, you are crazy." Reid shook his head as he watched Audrey stand and stretch, then start walking toward the creek.

Connor laughed out loud causing him to choke on his own food.

Reid slapped him on the back, maybe a little harder than needed, to help him dislodge the food. Moments later, when Connor could form words again, he glared at his brother.

"Well, I *may* be crazy. That's not really the point. Besides, I didn't mean for myself. I was thinking of someone else who could use a woman around his house."

Reid felt Connor's eyes on him.

"I don't need a woman around my house. I'm fine on my own." He wanted to put an end to this discussion now.

"You may not need a woman but Sophia does. It isn't fair for her to be left without someone to care for her. You can't keep relying on the help of Ma or Ella and now that Phoebe and Grace will be moving into their own house, you need someone to help you." Connor stopped talking but Reid could tell he wasn't finished.

"Do you think we haven't all noticed how much you avoid spending time with her? She's your daughter Reid and she deserves to have her daddy close giving her the love she needs. You're all she has left." Connor was the youngest but he was also the one who wasn't afraid to say it like it was.

"I don't avoid her." Reid kicked at a stone laying in the dirt. "I just don't know how to care for a child, and..." He couldn't speak the rest of what he'd been thinking.

But Connor wasn't backing down. "And what?"

He shot his brother a glare that would have sent most people running. Connor sat staring back at him.

"And, every time I look at her, I'm reminded of Eliza and how she died." He stood up angrily with his fists clenched. "Is that what you wanted to hear? I know you are all worried about me, and only want what's best for me, but I'm fine and I will do what I have to do to care for my daughter. I don't need some woman messing with things."

He moved to storm off but a scream and a loud splash caught his attention. He immediately recognized Sophia's voice and his heart plummeted. His feet were moving before he even had time to think.

He raced past the others who all stood to see what the commotion was but he felt like everything was moving too slow as he tried to get to the spot where the scream had come from.

He raced down the bank and around a large tree and was shocked to see Audrey in the middle of the creek, water up to her waist, dress drenched right through and her bonnet hanging limply from her neck.

She held Sophia in her arms; his daughter was crying and clinging to Audrey for her life. He heard Audrey's voice as she soothed the child. "It's all right, sweetheart. I've got you."

He raced out into the thigh-high water and took the terrified child out of Audrey's arms, holding her tight in one arm while taking the woman's hand in the other.

Once they reached dry land, he couldn't hold back the emotion.

"What the hell happened?" The words came out much angrier than he'd meant but he couldn't shake the fear that gripped him when he saw the two of them out in the water.

Audrey stood there before him, shivering. Thankfully, Ella had thought to grab a blanket from the picnic area when she saw what was happening.

She wrapped the blanket around Audrey. Everyone else was fussing around them, asking if everyone was all right.

"I just came down for a bit of a walk, to stretch my legs...when I came around the corner, I saw Sophia had crawled out onto that rock that juts over the creek just there." Her voice trembled as she looked up at Reid with fear in her eyes. Her black hair hung in wet curls around her face.

"She was chasing after a butterfly. I didn't want to scare her because she was already right at the edge, so I just ran. She fell in before I could reach her." She choked on her words as the memories flashed across her pale face. "I know the water isn't very deep, but I knew it was too deep for her. I got to her as fast as I could!" Reid peered down into eyes filled with concern.

He took Sophia in his arms and checked her for injury. Other than being completely soaked, she appeared unharmed. Her bottom lip trembled as she tried to stop crying.

"Sophia, you know you aren't supposed to go off on your own." He tried to keep the anger from his own voice but he needed to let the child know she'd done wrong so she wouldn't do it again.

At the sound of her father's voice, she started crying loudly again. Audrey reached up, caressing the back of her head. "Shhhh...it's all right, sweetheart. Your daddy isn't mad, he was just scared. You need to listen to him so you don't get hurt."

Sophia tucked her head into Reid's shoulder, knowing she was in trouble. Reid glanced at the small woman who had jumped into the creek to save his daughter. She met his eyes. He noticed her cheeks go red and she pulled her hand back as though it had been burned.

"I'm sorry. I just hate to hear her cry." She lowered her face and pulled the blanket tight around her trembling shoulders.

"That's all right." He swallowed hard, feeling uncomfortable at the closeness. "Thank you for jumping in after her. She's a bit of a minx." He felt terrible that he hadn't been watching his daughter close enough. "I should have done a better job of watching over her."

Audrey looked up at him and shrugged. "You can't watch them every minute of the day. It's easy for children to slip away. I'm just glad I was there to pull her out of the water."

The other women clicked and muttered over Audrey like mother hens, pulling her back toward the picnic area. She turned back to Reid and smiled. He didn't move from that spot as he watched her walk away. Sophia wriggled in his arms but his mother lifted the child from his embrace and hugged her close, soothing her tears as only a woman can.

Now that the excitement was over, the crowd dispersed, returning to the picnic. He finally let out the breath he hadn't even realized he was holding.

"Told you she was nice." Connor slapped him hard on the back, winking as he followed the others back up the bank, leaving Reid standing there alone.

Maybe his brother wasn't so wrong, after all.

CHAPTER 3

"I knew my father wasn't going to let me stay. Now that he knows I'm no longer married, he is insisting I uphold the contract he signed with the Hillman's." Audrey sat down beside Phoebe on the bench outside the O'Hara's mercantile. She reread the letter her father sent. It felt like the air had been knocked from her lungs.

"Did he say when he'd be here?" Her friend's voice carried sadness at hearing she would be leaving. Audrey understood that sadness. She didn't want to leave here either.

Audrey glared down at the paper in her hands, trying to see the words through the tears that were threatening to fall.

She read aloud:

"Dear Daughter,

I am saddened to hear of Pete's passing, but perhaps now you will come to your senses and fulfill the duty of marriage that had been arranged for you in the first place. You have had your fun, trekking across the country chasing some need for adventure, but now you need to grow up and do what is expected of you.

Thankfully for you, Frank Hillman has been very patient and understanding about the whole situation, and has agreed to carry through with the marriage as planned. You are fortunate that he is so generous.

We will be coming for you immediately, and we expect you to be ready to come back to Kentucky when we arrive.

I hope this little adventure has opened your eyes to the realities of life and the harshness of the world. You have an obligation to uphold your agreement to marry into the Hillman family.

Letting you make the journey on your own isn't something we trust you to do. You can expect us within the next few weeks.

Sincerely,

Your Father"

Her hands shook and she couldn't even lift her eyes to face Phoebe. "They are leaving to come and take me back to Kentucky, which means they will already be on their way. So I have a few weeks left here, at most."

"Is everything all right dear?" Susan O'Hara's

voice cut through the silence that had fallen over the women on the bench.

Audrey glanced up and offered the kind woman a smile. "Just a letter from my father. They are coming to take me back to Kentucky."

"Oh my! Why on earth would they do that?" She sat down on the other side of Audrey and put her arm around the young woman's shoulders. "Surely they must know you're making your home here?"

Audrey shrugged, unsure she could explain the complexities of her situation to the other woman. "I was supposed to marry another man, Frank Hillman. But I ran off and married Pete. The Hillman family is high up on the society ladder in Kentucky and marrying him was supposed to be some great honor." She paused, letting her gaze take in the breathtaking hills and trees surrounding this small community she had grown to love. She heard the sound of laughter from the townsfolk talking next to a wagon parked outside the feed mill. She heard horses' hooves making their way up the street, pulling wagons full of people who smiled and waved as they plodded past.

She sighed and folded the letter up, then placed it back in the envelope. "It never mattered that I didn't want to marry him. I never fit in with the other society ladies and I was never attracted to Frank. He is handsome but he has no personality at all. Besides, my heart already belonged to Pete."

"But surely if he knew you were in love with Pete, he wouldn't have forced you to marry against your will?" Susan just couldn't understand. On their way west, they had spent long hours talking and she had told Audrey how poor she had grown up. Marriage among high society members would never make sense to her. It didn't make sense to Audrey either but, unfortunately, she had no other choice.

"Yes, he would have. And, now that Pete's gone, I am expected to uphold the deal my father made for me to marry Frank. As the oldest daughter, it is expected of me. If I had money of my own or a way to support myself, I could fight it, but..." She bowed her head and blinked at her hands still tightly gripping the letter.

"Pete and I had nothing other than a few possessions. And, there aren't many paying jobs for a woman on her own out here. Mrs. Larsen has been wonderful, letting me earn enough to have a place to live and a little extra to get by but it isn't enough to build a life on."

"But Audrey, you can't go back to Kentucky. This is your home now. We will find a way for you to stay." Phoebe reached out and took one of Audrey's hands. "Especially since you are about to become a godmother."

The words sank in and she whipped her head up to gaze at her friend, her heart full of joy for Phoebe. "You're having a baby?" She couldn't help the smile that spread across her face when her friend nodded. She grabbed Phoebe in a bear hug and squealed.

"Oh Phoebe! I am so happy for you and Colton!" She pulled back and let Mrs. O'Hara put her arms around Phoebe, too. Susan had been like a mother to them both during the trip west and her affection for the girls continued even after they settled in Bethany.

"This is wonderful news, Phoebe!" She jumped from her seat and ran toward the front door of the mercantile. "James! We are going to be grandparents!"

It didn't matter that Phoebe wasn't her daughter, she had already decided this baby would be her grandchild. Audrey smiled and watched the woman race into the mercantile to tell her husband the great news.

"Sorry, I know this isn't likely the best time to tell you, when you have your own burdens. But, I hope it will give you a reason to at least try to stay." Audrey peered into Phoebe's tearful eyes.

"I wish I could, Phoebe. I really do. But, I just don't see how." Audrey stood and began to pace. The dust kicked into the air by a passing wagon flew into her eyes but she didn't even notice. Her eyes were already stinging with unshed tears. "I love it here. It feels like home. I know it sounds silly but I feel like I'm still close to Pete here, knowing it's where we would have built our lives together. But, I know my father and he won't give up. He is angry that I didn't go through with the wedding to Frank. There's no way he will listen to reason now and let me stay here, especially since I can't make a living."

"Why do you ladies look like your dog just died?" Colton came out of the mercantile with his arms piled high with bags of flour and other necessities they needed to make the move into their new home. He glanced at Phoebe. "I thought you were telling her the exciting news? She doesn't seem as happy as I'd imagined."

Reid was right behind him, his own arms piled with items to put in the wagon. Phoebe had mentioned they had all came in to town together, leaving Sophia and Grace back at their mother's for the day. Reid's eyes found the two women, his gaze landing on Audrey. Her cheeks warmed under his scrutiny and she tried to shake her head clear.

"Everything all right?" He directed his question at Audrey. She still stood in front of the bench, holding the letter that suddenly felt like it weighed a hundred pounds. Reid nodded to it. "Bad news from back home?"

He really didn't waste time on useless words. She had to smile because even though she knew he was gruff on the outside, she sensed there was way more going on inside.

"Audrey's father is coming to get her and take

her back to Kentucky to marry a man he has arranged for her." Phoebe blurted the words out before Audrey had a chance to speak.

Both men just stared at her, shocked. Finally, Reid broke the heavy silence.

"I assume by the look on your face you aren't happy with the news." Reid kept his eyes on Audrey as he moved to set the food in his arms onto the back of the wagon. "Why don't you just tell him you want to stay here if that's what you want?"

"I would like to stay but it isn't that simple. My father says I have an obligation to marry the man he had originally arranged for me and, unfortunately, I don't have many other options." She swallowed hard, wishing Colton and Reid weren't there to witness her unhappiness. She liked to believe she was a strong woman, coming out to Oregon on her own after losing her husband, but the truth was she was still fearful and insecure.

She worried about her safety because as a woman out West, with no family, she was at the mercy of anyone who sought to take advantage of her. She also knew she might not earn enough money to survive on her own. Her dream of having a farm where she could grow her own garden and keep her own house was never going to come true without Pete, so the only option she had at the moment was the one she'd run away from all those months ago.

"It won't be all bad. Frank seems like a nice enough man. And, I will have all of the best ball gowns and anything else my heart desires." She put on a weak smile to convince herself and the others of the truth of her words. Reid just lifted an eyebrow, his disbelief clear.

By now, Susan had returned with James in tow to congratulate Phoebe but they stopped in their celebration to listen to Audrey's words.

James walked to Audrey and put his arm around her shoulder. "You know you are always welcome to stay with us, dear. You don't need to go home with your father if you don't want to. We will find a way to help you."

Audrey smiled at the kind man who always looked out for them all. "I know you would do that for me, Mr. O'Hara, but I can't rely on your charity." She still called him Mr. O'Hara even though he always insisted she call him James.

A silence fell over the group outside the store.

"Listen, my father isn't here yet, so we don't need to say goodbye already." She desperately wanted to have a reason to smile at the moment.

"Besides, I just found out my best friend is having a baby. I think that calls for a celebration."

"Audrey's right. I think what we need is a night of dancing and fun, just like we used to do out on the trail!" Susan clapped her hands together in excitement.

Audrey smiled at Reid, hoping he'd return it. As expected, he just stood there staring at her, his face hard and joyless. Colton picked Phoebe up from the bench and swung her around while she laughed.

"Well, I reckon a party to celebrate our new home, a baby on the way, and to give Audrey the perfect send off is in order, then!"

And with that, a party was planned for the coming Saturday at Colton and Phoebe's new house. Audrey was excited but felt a sadness in her heart. It would be the last get together with all of the people she'd begun to see as family.

Reid never said a word, listening to the others' plan, excitement filling their voices, but Audrey noticed he kept his eyes on her. She was uncomfortable under his scrutiny, as though he could see right through her fake smile to the sadness in her heart.

She guessed, because he'd lost someone he loved too, he could recognize another's sadness even when they tried to pretend otherwise.

Shaking off her discomfort and weariness, she turned to plan with the others.

For now, she was still here and she intended to enjoy what little time was left.

She would worry about everything else after the party.

CHAPTER 4

Reid leaned against the tree, watching the couples move around in the clearing they set up for dancing. Lanterns hung from trees, illuminating the area with a bright glow. Long tables were filled with every kind of food imaginable. The night was starting cool but no one seemed to notice.

It was as though the entire settlement of Bethany had shown up. If there was one thing he knew about this community, it was how much they loved a good celebration. Living out here, completely reliant on the land to provide for them, they knew much hardship so parties like this were the only way to relieve the stresses of life.

The sounds of a fiddle filled the evening sky and voices joined together in cheerful song filled his ears.

But still, he didn't join in. His eyes found his daughter who was being spun around in her uncle Logan's arms. Her smile lit up her whole face, reminding him so much of her mother.

He dropped his gaze quickly, shaking his thoughts free of the memory. Every time he looked at his daughter, he was reminded of Eliza. Though it had now been almost two years since she died, the wound was still raw.

"Sophia's having fun." The sound of Audrey's voice startled him.

"Sorry, I didn't mean to sneak up on you." She gave him one of her smiles that never quite reached her eyes.

"That's all right. " He put his hands into his front pockets and leaned against the tree again. "How come you aren't out there dancing with the others?"

She pulled her shawl around her shoulders and turned to watch the people dancing in the light of the lanterns. Silence stretched between them. Finally, she offered a slight shrug. "I didn't really feel like dancing." She met his gaze. "It's hard when you miss the one person you want to dance with the most."

They held the stare between them as two people who understood the loneliness of loss even when surrounded by loved ones.

He didn't know what to say to her, to help ease her pain, so he decided to change the subject. "So, any word on when your father will arrive?" Seeing her grimace, he wished he could take the words back.

"No, not yet. I'm sure he will be here soon, though." She sounded defeated.

He felt bad for bringing up a subject that upset her. He wanted to make her feel better. Before he knew what he was doing, he reached out to her. "I'm not much of a dancer, but maybe it would do us both good to give it a try."

Audrey stared at him with her mouth half open. He watched, his breath stuck in his throat, as she pulled her bottom lip in between her teeth and bit down as though in deep thought.

Finally, she nodded and put her hand in his. "It's been awhile since I've danced but I'll do my best to keep from scuffing your boots." Her eyes held a bit of a sparkle he'd never seen before.

He led her out to where the others were dancing while trying to avoid the curious glances from his family. He knew they were all surprised to see him taking part in the fun. He hadn't seen much reason to celebrate in the past few years so he'd usually just stand and watch rather than participate.

The music was lively so he swung Audrey around in time, matching the movement of the other dancers. As they danced a smile lit up her face and he felt a small tug on his heart when he realized he was genuinely glad to give her this bit of happiness before her father arrived to take her from Bethany.

He'd met Audrey soon after his brother, Colton, arrived with the wagon train he'd been hired to lead out here to Oregon. Reid knew how hard it must be for her to face the sorrow of losing everything she'd dreamt of when she left with her husband to come west. His gaze met hers and he saw the underlying sadness she was desperately trying to hide.

He could see that she was having fun but he also saw her eyes watching the people she had grown to love and was now saying good-bye to. It was clear that she was trying to make everyone believe she was having more fun than her heart would really allow.

He understood the feeling well.

But, as they spun around under the trees, he realized *he* was actually having a good time. It was something he hadn't experienced in a very long time. Caring for a child on his own, while grieving the loss of someone he loved, had taken its toll on him.

"Is that a smile I see on your face?" Audrey's voice cut into his thoughts. "I've always wondered what you would look like if you smiled." She grinned up at him.

"I've been known to smile from time to time." He spun her out in a quick turn, enjoying her chirp of laughter. She spun back in and she stepped on his boot. "I thought you said you would keep your feet away from my boots?"

"I'm sorry. I never made any promises." She laughed again, a heady, delightful sound.

The song came to an end and he led her to the table where they were offered lemonade and punch. He poured a glass for each of them.

"It's been awhile since I've had that much fun. Thank you for dusting off your boots to dance with me." Audrey took a sip from her glass.

Logan approached holding Sophia and handed the small girl to Reid. Once he'd passed him the child, he extended his hand to Audrey and bowed. "Now that my older, grumpier brother has dragged you out there and tromped all over your pretty little toes, I believe it's time to let the more handsome brother show you how it's really done."

Audrey let Logan pull her back out for a dance and the sound of her laughter reached his ears. He turned his attention to where James O'Hara spun Susan around in his arms with surprising agility. Even old Harlan from the mill was on his best behavior tonight, taking Dorothy Larsen for a whirl around the makeshift outdoor dance floor.

Sophia snuggled into his shoulder. She'd be

asleep before long. It was well past her bedtime, so he was surprised she'd hung on as long as she had. She was getting around well on her own now and had been dancing with everyone.

He sighed and decided it was time to get her home. He tipped his glass back to finish his drink but before he could swallow the last sip, Connor came up behind him and slapped him hard on the back. Sputtering, he turned to glare at his youngest brother.

"You could warn people when sneaking up on them. I could have dropped Sophia." he exclaimed, anger heating his words. Sophia lifted her head and smiled at Connor, then promptly closed her eyes again and snuggled back into her father for warmth.

"Well, I had to see if you'd given any thought to what we talked about. I saw you dancing with Audrey. You looked like you were enjoying yourselves." He leaned against a tree, putting his knee up and resting his foot on the trunk.

"We were just dancing, Connor. Doesn't mean I'm ready to get married." He shifted uneasily.

What did his brother know about anything? He wasn't even fully grown himself.

"Listen, Reid. I know you think I'm too young to understand much about love or marriage or anything like that. And, you're likely right. But, I do know when someone needs help. I hate that you've gone through so much over the last two years. I watched a part of you die with Eliza. You've carried your grief and your guilt like a shield, not letting anyone else in." He paused waiting for Reid to meet his gaze.

"I *am* old enough to see a man when he is lonely and to understand when a child needs a woman to help care for her. There aren't many women around these parts and Audrey would make any man a fine wife." They both glanced out to where Logan was twirling the woman in his arms. "And if *you* don't see it, I'm mighty sure someone else will."

Connor walked away, leaving him alone again. Reid just stood, holding his daughter in his arms, listening to her breathe softly as she slept. But his eyes were focused on the woman they had been talking about.

Reid knew it was common practice for people out here to marry for more practical reasons than love but he had a hard time believing it was the best choice for him. He could never offer Audrey his heart. Eliza took that with her when she died.

But, he also knew that Audrey, of all people, would understand that. He knew she'd left part of her heart on the trail beside her husband Pete's grave.

Maybe the two of them *would* be good for each other.

He could offer her the chance to stay here, where she was happy, and give her a good life. She could help him raise Sophia and tend to his home, taking some of the burden off his own shoulders.

"Reid? Did you hear me?" Audrey's voice broke through his thoughts. He hadn't even realized the dance was over. He'd been absently watching Connor throw his sister Ella around playfully in a dance and didn't notice the woman from his thoughts approach him.

"Sorry. I didn't hear you come up." He felt heat rise in his cheeks as though he'd been caught thinking about something forbidden. He knew it was foolish, that she couldn't possibly know what he was thinking, but he couldn't shake the embarrassment.

"I said, I could take Sophia for you and lay her down in Phoebe's house so you can enjoy the party some more. I'm a bit tired but, by the looks of it, James and Susan won't be ready to head back into town any time soon." She waved her hand toward the older couple she'd rode out to the party with. They were still dancing. "I'll gladly lie down with Sophia."

In that moment, he knew he needed to ask her. Would she accept his proposal? Accept him?

"Here, I'll walk up to the house with you." He began walking and she kept pace beside him.

Once they were just out of sight of the dancers, he stopped. The night was well lit, with the faint glow still shining from the lanterns at the party and the light from the moon was so bright, they could see for miles. It was easy to see the hills in the distance, through the trees in the yard, and just then the lone hoot of an owl reached their ears as they stood in the stillness.

He turned to Audrey, her face a mask of confusion. "Is everything all right, Reid?"

He felt like a schoolboy, unsure how to speak to a girl.

He cleared his throat and reached up with his free hand to remove his hat. Sophia still slept soundly, tucked into his shoulder, unaware of what was happening around her.

"I'm not really sure how to say this and I'm more than likely going to mess things up pretty bad..."

Audrey reached out and placed her hand on his arm, her brows furrowed in worry. "Reid, what is it? What's the matter?"

"Well, you know I have been raising Sophia by myself and, truthfully, it hasn't been easy. I lost Eliza and I don't imagine I could ever love another woman again but I also understand the need for companionship and for someone to help care for my daughter. I know I don't have much to offer, certainly not the riches of the man you're to marry back in Kentucky, but I could offer you a home and a family. If you want it." He stood there, swallowing hard as he realized the extent of his botched proposal.

Audrey just stood there staring at him, with her mouth hanging partway open.

He slapped his hat against his leg and gazed down at his boots. This wasn't going as he'd planned. He wished she'd say something to help him know what she was thinking.

"What are you saying, Reid?" She spoke slowly as though she wasn't quite sure she had heard him right.

"I'm saying, maybe you could stay here and marry me. It seems it would solve both of our problems; you could stay here in Bethany and I would have someone to help me with my daughter." He finally met her gaze. He knew most women liked flowery words, professing how much they were loved, but he couldn't give that to Audrey.

"I can't promise you anything more than companionship. We could be married, no strings attached, until we get to know one another better. I want you to know, though, that I am not offering my heart and I don't expect to take the place of Pete in your heart, either."

Why wasn't she saying anything? Reid knew everything was coming out wrong but he didn't want her to have false ideas of what their marriage would be —if she accepted.

"You're asking me to marry you?" She asked

incredulously as she stood before him as stiff as a board.

"I know it's sudden and bad timing with your father coming to get you and all." He swallowed hard, trying to soothe his suddenly dry throat. "But, if you will have me, Audrey, yes, I am asking you to marry me."

CHAPTER 5

A
udrey glanced around the room to make sure she had everything packed. She'd sold most of the bigger personal items at the fort during the journey to Bethany, including her wagon, coming the rest of the way in Phoebe's. When she finally arrived in Oregon, she had only her clothes and a few smaller belongings.

She paused and thought back on the last few days. It was all a whirlwind in her mind.

After Reid asked her to marry him, it took her only moments to answer. She knew, in her heart, it was the solution she had prayed for.

And, if she were completely honest with herself, seeing Reid standing before her so vulnerable and unsure of himself, had touched her. She knew how much he'd grieved for his wife and she knew it hadn't been easy for him to ask her to marry him. He was doing what he could for his daughter.

Also, the fact that he didn't expect anything more from her than she was ready to give, helped too. She knew he understood the sadness she still carried in her own heart.

Together, they could offer each other company. He was giving her a way to stay in Oregon, to have the home she'd always dreamed of having, far away from the society life in Kentucky.

And, in return, she could help him raise his beautiful little girl and take care of his home.

She tried to shake off her guilty feelings over remarrying so soon. She hoped Pete would understand, that he'd want her to have a chance at happiness again.

But, deep down, even though she tried to let on she wasn't bothered, she *did* feel guilty. She didn't know if she was ready to say goodbye to that part of her life with Pete and, by remarrying, she worried that was exactly what she was doing.

She held the handmade jewelry box in her hand, trying to feel connected to the man who had given it to her. She didn't want him to think she'd already moved on or that what they had together hadn't mattered to her.

"Are you ready to go?" Reid stood in the doorway of her now empty room looking as nervous as she felt.

She took one last glance around the room and then bent to pick up the small bag by her feet. Reid crouched and picked it up before she could.

"Did you want to put that in the bag?" He nodded toward the box she still held. "It looks like it might mean an awful lot to you. Wouldn't want it getting broken."

She ran her fingers over the lid's smooth surface. "Pete made this for me as a wedding gift." Immediately, she felt bad for sharing something so intimate with the man she was supposed to marry later that day. Her gaze flew to his face.

"I'm sorry."

His eyes never left the box but a gentle smile curved his lips.

"It's fine, Audrey. I don't expect you to never talk about Pete or the life you had before me." He reached out, taking the box from her. He stared at it for a few minutes more before tucking it safely inside the pocket of the bag he held.

He offered her his arm and she took it, looping her arm behind his and placing her hand along his forearm. "Are you ready to get married?" She sensed that he was trying to make light of something that made them both nervous.

She smiled up at him. "Thank you for giving me the chance to stay here and make a home with you." The words didn't fully express the depth of her gratitude.

He nodded. "I wish I could offer you more. You deserve to have someone who can love you. But, for now, I think we will be able to make a good home for Sophia and you can stay here, living where you are happy." He chuckled deep in his throat. "And besides, you may not be thanking me much after having to live with me for a while."

She appreciated the fact he was trying to calm her nerves. Everything was happening so fast but she knew it was the right thing. Her father was going to be terribly angry when he got there but she'd be married and there'd be nothing he could do about it.

So, before the morning church service, they would say their vows in front of their friends and family. In just over a week, she'd gone from thinking she was going home to marry a man her father had chosen for her, to marrying a man she'd chosen, but still didn't know much about. Other than the fact he would never be able to love her.

They arrived at the wagon and he set her bag in the back, then turned to help her up onto the seat. This man, someone she'd known only a short time, was about to become her husband. He was dressed in the clothes she had seen him wear to church, a brown jacket over top of a white cotton shirt. He wore a clean, wide-brimmed hat and his boots were a bit scuffed from wear but were cleaned and polished.

She wished she had something beautiful to wear. She'd grown up wearing the most stunning ball gowns and fancy dresses but the day she had married Pete, she wore a simple, plain dress, one she'd take with her on the journey west. Wearing a fancy dress for her wedding to Pete wasn't an option since they had married quickly in the camp settlement before the wagon train set out.

And now, all she owned were a few worn and tattered dresses she'd brought west with her. She'd worn them through the trail dust, over mountains, and river crossings. She was wearing her best one but she was embarrassed at the state it was in.

As if reading her thoughts, Reid put his hand out for her to take. "I know it isn't much but I wanted to give you something before we headed to the church." He shuffled uneasily as their eyes met.

"I figured you likely wouldn't have much to wear, and it isn't near as fancy as what you would be wearing if you were headed back home for your wedding day, but I wanted you to have something nice..."

She smiled at his attempt to string the sweet words together. She appreciated that he even thought he had to get her a gift at all.

He let go of her hand, then turned and pulled a box down from the wagon seat. He held it out and nodded for her to open it. She pulled off the lid and pushed the paper aside.

Inside was the most beautiful, delicate fabric she had ever seen. She pulled it out and immediately recognized a shawl she had admired in the mercantile in town. She gently caressed the fabric between her fingers, unable to find the words to express how much she loved it.

"I would have liked to get you a beautiful dress to wear today but I didn't really know your size and there isn't much to choose from at the O'Hara's store. But, when I saw this, I thought it would suit you." Reid was obviously uncomfortable, speaking faster than usual, unsure how she would react to the gift.

Tears burned at the back of her eyes and she doubted her ability to speak. A lump formed in her throat at the thoughtfulness of the gesture. She lifted her gaze to his and smiled at the genuine kindness she saw there. She knew, without a doubt, she was doing the right thing by marrying him.

"Thank you, Reid. You didn't have to get me anything." He shrugged as though it wasn't a big deal, then turned and set the box in the wagon. He reached over and removed the tattered shawl she wore around her shoulders, draping it over the wagon seat, then took the new one from her hands and wrapped it gently around her shoulders. He stood back and smiled. "You look lovely."

She smiled. Three simple words and he couldn't even begin to know how much they meant. But, to her, they were priceless. They made her feel beautiful. She needed that, especially today.

She put her hand into his and let him help her up onto the seat. They drove to the church in silence, both lost in their own thoughts. Many emotions made their way into Audrey's heart and she glanced at Reid more than once.

I will never forget you, Pete. Please don't be angry with me for marrying another man. I can't go back to Kentucky and Reid is a good man. He seems like someone you would have liked... The thoughts kept running through her mind and the short ride to the church was over before she knew it.

Reid reached up and helped her down, lifting her by the waist. He set her down but hesitated to remove his hands. Other wagons pulled up and voices called out in greeting all around them. But, his eyes never left hers. "Are you sure? It's not too late to change your mind." His lips turned up in a half smile and she was sure that, through the silence between them, she heard her heart beating.

"I'm sure." He let out a heavy breath and nodded before letting go of her waist. Their strangely intimate moment was interrupted as excited well wishers and family arrived to celebrate the small wedding taking place before Sunday church services.

In what seemed like mere minutes, she was standing before the minister, at the front of the church, facing Reid. She felt as though she were watching the ceremony unfold from somewhere outside of her own body and the words were coming from far away. Not more than a year ago, she'd recited these same vows to Pete and, now, she was saying them to another man.

When it was her turn to speak her vows, she swallowed hard. Reid was watching her with concern, holding her hands tight in his. She tried to focus on the present, feeling the blisters and calluses on his work-worn hands and when she thought she was surely going to faint, he smiled at her, gently squeezing her fingers.

She smiled back, then repeated the vows that would tie them together for life. He said his words quietly, just loud enough for her and the minister to hear. A small part of her wished their vows were being spoken in love.

She knew she was marrying a good man and, sometimes, love wasn't necessary. She'd been lucky enough to know love once and now she could be happy to have someone to care about and who she knew would care for her. Even if he couldn't love her.

For now, it was enough.

CHAPTER 6

"**P**oor girl is tuckered out." Reid nodded to the tiny sleeping child Audrey held in her arms. She smiled down at her new daughter who yawned and fought to keep her eyes open. The ride from Reid's mother, Anna's, house hadn't taken long but Sophia hadn't stopped moving since she woke up that morning, so she was exhausted.

Everyone met at Anna's for their Sunday gathering after church. The weather held up, letting them spend the day outdoors even this late in the year. Many of the townsfolk joined them, happy for yet another chance to have some fun and, once again, Sophia spent the day playing and running around.

But now, they were headed home.

She'd ridden out to Reid's house after church a few times before to visit Phoebe while they stayed there but she hadn't paid much attention to the scenery on the drive out or the house itself other than to notice Reid wasn't much for decoration.

This time, she was arriving at her new home. Soon, she and Reid would be alone, in their house, with no interruptions. She shifted uncomfortably. He had said the marriage would have no strings attached, but was that possible in such an intimate space?

Would they sleep together? Apart?

She remembered that his house wasn't very big with just one bed in the back behind the centrally located fireplace. There was a table on the other side and a short row of cupboards. A narrow ladder beside the fireplace led up to a loft where, she assumed, Sophia would sleep when she was older.

"I tried to clean up as much as I could but it hasn't had a good cleaning since Phoebe moved to her own house. I admit I haven't taken much time to do any housekeeping."

"I'm sure it will be fine, Reid." She tried to keep the nervousness out of her voice.

They rode the rest of the way in silence. She admired the beauty of the land around them, hoping to let the scenery take her mind off the uneasiness she was feeling. She breathed in, taking the fresh air deep into her lungs. The sun was setting and, all around them, an orange glow illuminated the trees along the road.

They pulled up beside the house and Audrey took in the view of what was now her home. She'd always loved the rolling hills, trickling creek along the trees on the property, and the cozy front porch that looked out on the open fields.

Reid came around the wagon and reached up for Sophia. He tucked the child up under his shoulder, then lifted his hand to help Audrey down, too. She took his hand and reveled in the thought of being a part of this family.

"You're likely pretty tired. I will go in with you and we can tuck Sophia into her bed. Once I get your bags carried in, I'll go unhitch the horses and finish up the chores." They walked up the porch steps together.

The door creaked as he opened it and she stepped over the threshold making sure to take a good, long look. She noticed a few little touches she knew he meant to make her feel at home. There was a delicate flower-filled vase on the table and she was surprised to see the house wasn't as unkempt as he let on.

"I have a bed for Sophia down near my bed, so you can have the loft bed for now—it's to be Sophia's when she gets older. Grace had slept up there while they were here, looking after Sophia while I slept in the barn. I would take it and let you have my bed but my feet would be hanging over the edge." He was standing by the ladder leading up to the loft. "I know climbing a ladder to your bed isn't easy but I hope you can make do for now. I was thinking, maybe in the spring, we could add on a small room off the side or..." She heard the strain in his voice and knew how uncomfortable he was. She felt it, too.

"It will be perfect, Reid. Thank you for thinking of me. It will take us some time to get used to having one another around, I imagine, but for now, everything is just perfect." She offered him a reassuring smile she hoped conveyed her own nervousness.

They stood, staring at one another, unsure of what to do or what to say next. Finally, he nodded then turned and walked to the bedroom behind the fireplace. While he tucked Sophia in her bed, Audrey sat on one of the chairs by the table and ran her fingers along the smooth fabric of her new shawl.

"Sorry, I should have realized it would be chilly by the time we got home. I will get a fire going." He crouched down, throwing wood onto the hearth. Once he had a fire started, he stood and turned to face her.

"I will get your bags and you can unpack while I tend to the chores."

After bringing them all in and carrying them up for her, he left for the barn, leaving her alone in her new home.

She climbed the ladder to the loft. Overwhelmed with the reality of what had happened today, she sighed heavily.

She sat on the low bed in the cozy loft and pulled her knees to her chest, then wrapped her arms around them, resting her chin on top. She kept her gaze forward, taking in everything in the humble room.

There wasn't much in the space; besides the bed, there was a little table and a wardrobe—a bit big even for her meager belongings.

But the space was perfect. It was a far cry from her bedroom in Kentucky or the fancy house where she'd have been expected to entertain snobby society women if she had married Frank. But everything in this house was exactly what she'd always dreamed of having.

She swallowed hard, trying to push down the guilt that crept up whenever she thought about being happy, knowing it should have been with Pete.

She'd always wanted a family and now she had a little girl she could call her own. The thought of being a mother scared her a bit but Sophia was such a sweet child, it wouldn't be a hardship.

The scariest part was wondering how to be a wife to a man she didn't really know. Especially when they were both grieving losses in their lives.

She'd barely had time to be a wife to Pete, a man she had known as long as she could remember, so she didn't have much wifely experience to help her now.

The warmth of the fireplace soothed her so she laid down to rest her eyes for a few moments before unpacking. She rolled onto her side and closed her eyes. She only needed to rest for a moment...

REID REACHED OVER and tucked the sleeping woman into her new bed. He'd come back from doing the chores to the sound of silence in his house. He was used to the quiet but this time he had expected to hear Audrey moving about as she unpacked. Calling out to her softly so he didn't wake Sophia, he was surprised when she didn't reply.

Now, he knew why.

He couldn't make heads nor tails of this woman. She'd grown up surrounded by all of the finery she could ever want, yet she chose to live out here away from it all. He had noticed the few dresses she owned were worn, having been the only clothes she brought with her from Kentucky.

He felt bad that there wasn't enough time to get her even one nice dress to wear for the wedding but he planned to remedy her clothing situation soon. Whether she would let him or not was a different matter.

Audrey was always kind, gentle, and almost soft-spoken. But, there had been a few times a fire lit in her eyes and he had no doubt she had a temper—if the moment called for it. She had a stubborn streak and was unwilling to let anyone do something for her if she could do it herself.

He stood watching over her, his heart aching as she gave a quiet sigh and pulled the covers under her chin. He knew it was wrong to stare at her like this but he couldn't seem to tear his gaze away.

She really was beautiful. Her hair was dark and always seemed brushed to a bright sheen. Her skin was flawless and her lips were as red as the roses he had picked to place on the table welcoming her home. He'd always thought Eliza was the most stunning woman in the world but, looking down at the sleeping figure before him, he realized there were other kinds of beauty out there.

Guilt at his thoughts slammed into him. He ripped his gaze from Audrey and started back down the ladder. What was wrong with him? He owed Eliza his continued devotion especially since she had lost her life giving birth to their child.

He shouldn't ogle another woman even if that other woman happened to be his new wife.

He pushed his hands through his hair and sat on the chair facing the window that overlooked his land. It had been a long day and, even though he knew it was the right thing to do for Sophia, he still had misgivings about remarrying. He felt as though he were dishonoring Eliza's memory and his proposal to Audrey weighed heavily on his heart.

He heard the soft breathing of the woman in the loft through the quiet in his—their—house. It had been almost two years since a woman lived there.

He leaned his head back on the chair, closed his eyes, and rubbed the bridge of his nose. He listened to the sounds of the night outside and allowed his mind to drift off.

His thoughts drifted to Audrey. Tomorrow would be there before he knew it and it would be their first full day as husband and wife.

He didn't know if he was ready.

CHAPTER 7

The sound of metal hitting the floor startled Audrey as she bent to pull the biscuits from the oven. She turned and saw Sophia covered in eggs and the plate that had held them laying on the floor. The child's head dripped with egg yolk but her face was covered with a bright grin.

"Oh, you little goose. Why do I think you did that on purpose?" Audrey smiled and crouched down to pick the eggs up from the floor. The child laughed and clapped.

Before she could stand up, the door creaked open and footsteps moved across the floor. She lifted her head and noticed Reid moving through the doorway, looking at her with a hint of a smile on his face.

She stood quickly, hoping she didn't drop the plate a second time, and set the plate with the now ruined eggs on the table. Her nervous fingers worked to smooth the invisible wrinkles from her skirt. "This wee girl decided she didn't want her eggs, so I was just picking them up." She turned back to the stove, very nervous around her new husband.

He'd left early that morning with just a few words about completing the chores and returning for breakfast. Their first morning as a married couple was tense, both of them unsure how to act around the other.

She woke up that morning, mortified to find herself in the same dress she'd worn the day before. She remembered lying down and closing her eyes for just a moment and then waking up hours later with a blanket tucked up around her. Knowing Reid had to have found her that way, and then put the blanket on her, was humiliating. It was supposed to be their first evening together, talking and perhaps getting to know one another better, but she had ruined it by falling asleep.

That morning, when she'd awoken to him moving around downstairs and she'd come down the ladder, he surprised her when he acted as though nothing was wrong. He just informed her that he was heading out to do chores and that Sophia would likely sleep a bit longer after yesterday.

Now though, as she peeked back and noticed

him bend down to give his daughter's cheek a peck, uneasiness and uncertainty robbed her of words.

"Did you sleep all right last night? Were you warm enough?" His voice startled her and she dropped the plate of food she'd filled for him. His breakfast nearly splattered all over the stove. It wasn't a fancy wood stove like she'd seen in the kitchens back home but it was exactly how she had always imagined a farmhouse stove to look. Reid started the fire in it before leaving that morning, so she was able to make breakfast.

He walked up behind her and reached out to retrieve the plate. "Sorry, didn't mean to startle you."

He sat at the table beside Sophia who was seated in a small wooden chair. It looked like it was made just for her. It was table height, had a seat that folded out for her to sit in, and a little table top of her own.

Filling her own plate, she turned and sat at the table across from Reid. "No, that's all right. I'm just a bit jumpy this morning, I guess." She handed Sophia a piece of warm biscuit.

"I slept very well last night, thank you. I'm sorry for falling asleep; I was only planning to rest my eyes for a few moments." Her cheeks heated and she fought the urge to glance up at him.

"Well, I imagine you were pretty tired. Was a long day yesterday, with a lot of new things to face. I tucked myself in only a few minutes after coming in from the barn." She lifted her head and watched him take a bite of his breakfast.

"I'm not sure what you did but these biscuits are delicious." He offered her a smile.

"Thanks. I wasn't really supposed to be doing any cooking back home because we had a cook who took care of that for us. But, I used to sneak into the kitchen whenever I could and our cook taught me everything she knew." She wasn't afraid to tell him what she'd done. He wasn't like the people back home who would have perished at the thought.

He nodded, then popped another piece of biscuit in his mouth. "I can tell."

They continued eating, listening to Sophia as she chattered non-stop in her own language, laughing and making cute noises. More than once, Audrey had to reach down and pick something up Sophia dropped. It became a fun game, with Sophia squealing in delight every time Audrey handed the dropped item back to her.

"I have to head into town today if you would like to come. I was thinking we could visit O'Hara's mercantile and see what fabrics they have for sale. Maybe you could find something you can use to make yourself a nice dress or two." She read discomfort in his expression but she appreciated his thoughtfulness.

"I would love to come and I wouldn't mind,

perhaps, making a few curtains as well, if that's all right with you. Just to add something to your home." She immediately felt terrible, hoping he wouldn't think she thought his home inadequate.

He paused and looked around the sparsely decorated room, then nodded. "I would imagine a few curtains could make things homier in here." He set his fork down and stared at her for a few seconds before continuing. "And, it isn't just my home anymore, remember that. This is your home now too, Audrey. So, any changes you want to make, or sprucing up you want to do, you're welcome to do it. We may not be married in the conventional sense but I appreciate you agreeing to help me out with Sophia, so your comfort is important to me."

A butterfly fluttered through her insides.

It was her home, too. Her new family.

She knew it had to be difficult for him to let another woman share the home he had built for his first wife, the woman he loved and mourned daily. His willingness to let her make his house a bit more *her* home lifted her spirits.

"Thank you for that, Reid. I appreciate it." Though things were still awkward between them, she hoped they'd become more at ease with one another. Today was definitely a great start.

THE RIDE into town was lovely. They dropped Sophia off with Phoebe, then rode to town together in the wagon. Along the way, Reid pointed out the land he worked with his brothers, the tree that had been struck by lightning twice last summer, the road that led to Walter Jenkins's farm, where Ella worked with his horses, and many other sights that he thought would interest her.

She'd enjoyed the ride immensely, realizing that Reid could carry on a conversation, if the mood struck him. She was getting to know more about the land where she now lived and the people who made up the settlement around Bethany.

They pulled up in front of the mercantile and she smiled at Susan O'Hara who was standing out on the front step waving her arm as though she hadn't seen Audrey in days.

"How is the newly married couple?" Susan beamed and if a person didn't know any better, they'd think she was Audrey's own mother. "I'm surprised to see you in town today." She walked over to the wagon as Reid came around to reach up and help Audrey down.

"Well, we needed to pick up a few things so we thought we would spend some time together on the ride in." Reid smiled up at Audrey, obviously not as uncomfortable as she was about what Susan was insinuating they *should* be doing.

Reid set Audrey down on the ground in front of

him and turned to Susan. "I have to head up to the feed store. Can you help Audrey find some fabric for new dresses and anything else she needs?"

With that, he hopped back into the wagon and headed up the street.

"So, my dear, come in here and tell me everything. " Susan practically dragged her into the store.

"Susan, you are going to pull my arm right off." Audrey joked, lovingly.

"Oh, I'm so sorry. I was thinking about you all night, hoping you were happy. I know how hard it must be marrying again so soon after losing your love." Susan patted Audrey's arm before letting go and walking behind the counter.

"It was fine, Susan. My first night with Reid was a bit awkward and I was uncertain how we should act. Even though I've known Reid in the weeks since we have been here, we haven't really spent much time talking and certainly not alone. So, I'm still a bit nervous and unsure of how things will go. But he is a nice man and he is kind to me." Susan stared at her for a moment, then nodded and walked to the table covered with bolts of fabric.

She set a few out for Audrey to look at and, before she knew it, an hour had passed. During that time, she visited with the other woman and chose fabrics that would make simple, sturdy dresses for her and Sophia. She'd picked a spritely yellow gingham for curtains. She hoped Reid would like them.

She also noticed a bright, blue checkered fabric that she knew would be handsome on Reid. Susan wrapped the fabric in paper so Reid wouldn't see it. Audrey wanted to make a shirt out of it, maybe a birthday present. But she suddenly realized she didn't even know something as simple as when her husband's birthday even was.

She mentioned it to Susan. "Don't be too hard on yourself. The wedding came suddenly. The friendship will come in time dear, just be patient. You both have your own feelings to work through and I think that you can help each other heal. You couldn't find a nicer man than Reid Wallace, so just give yourself the time you need to get to know one another."

The sound of the bell tinkling above the door interrupted them. She turned and saw Reid enter the store. "Did you find everything you needed, Audrey?" He reached out to lift the pile of fabric Susan had wrapped. The paper would protect the new fabric from getting dusty on the way back to the homestead.

Susan winked at Audrey when Reid picked up the last package. That one held the fabric for his shirt. "She got everything she needed Reid and then some."

Reid raised an eyebrow, then must've decided

not to ask what she meant. "Just put it all on my tab, Susan."

The older woman followed them to the door to say her farewell.

They stepped outside and turned to follow the sound of horses coming up the street. The pounding of the horses' hooves was a common sound around the town but the faint jingling of bells was out of place.

Reid set the fabric on the seat of the wagon and Audrey put her hand up to shield her eyes, her gaze moving to see who was headed their direction.

"Well, I wonder who that could be, pulling into our humble town with such fine looking horses?" Susan stood in awe as the fancy carriage came to a stop in front of the store.

Audrey knew that carriage, those horses. Her heart dropped into her stomach. She let out a small cry before she could stop herself and Reid rushed to her side. "Are you all right, Audrey?" His voice was full of concern.

She couldn't bring herself to reply. Her heart beat so loud, she heard the steady pounding in her own ears.

She knew who would climb from the carriage. And, soon, everyone else would, too.

CHAPTER 8

Reid glanced at Audrey's face and instantly knew something was wrong. In the time he'd known her, she always had a gentle smile on her face and a tenderness in her gaze that hid the strength she somehow contained in her petite body.

But now, as his gaze fell on her face, he saw fear. The smile was gone and her eyes were large and round, her brows furrowed between them. She trembled beneath his hand.

She didn't answer his gentle prodding so he pulled her to face him. "Audrey, what is it?" Her face was pale and her breathing shallow.

Before she could speak, the door to the carriage opened and a man half the size of Reid stepped out. Reid couldn't help but notice the short man's width was almost the same as his height. Why was Audrey so afraid of him?

"Hello, daughter. Imagine my surprise, finding you already! I thought for sure we would spend at least the first day trying to locate where you were trying to hide." The man cast his disapproving gaze around the dusty town. His lip turned up in a sneer.

"However, I can see now that it wouldn't have taken me more than a minute to find you in this filthy little village."

Reid listened to the pompous man speak, anger and surprise roiling through him. This was Audrey's father? With his hand at her back, he felt the tension in her body.

She didn't speak but the man moved toward her. As they watched, another man stepped out of the carriage, unfolding his legs and stretching his back as his feet hit the ground.

Reid tensed, sensing that this was the man Audrey was supposed to marry. He took his time digesting everything about the man before him. He couldn't help but compare himself, standing there in his dusty boots, worn pants, and badly bent hat. The other man's clothes were fine, clean, and probably cost more than Reid made in a year.

He was as tall as Reid and had hair as black as coal with a mustache to match. The man turned to face them and his lips turned up in a smile but something about the way he leered at Audrey sent a shiver down his spine.

"Father." Audrey gave the squat man a small hug,

their embrace stiff and awkward. "I had told you I would be fine here until the spring. You didn't need to come for me so soon." Her voice trembled.

"Well, Franklin didn't want to take the chance that you'd get cold feet again." Audrey's father pulled the other man over to stand next to him and patted him on the back. "We are fortunate that he has been so understanding and patient, after what you did running off with Pete Thomsen and all. You don't know how lucky you are that he is giving you another chance."

"Father, I wish you would have waited. I was going to send you another letter to tell you not to come..." Her voice trailed off and Reid felt terrible for the situation she was in. They knew her father and the day of reckoning was coming but he'd hoped she would have more time to prepare.

She lifted her gaze to his and something pulled at his heart. He wanted to somehow fix this but he knew her father wouldn't take the news of his daughter's new marriage well.

He knew he should say something to alleviate the weight on Audrey's shoulders. He put his hand out to the other man. He wanted to address him but he realized he didn't even know Audrey's maiden name, so he didn't know what to call her father.

"My name is Reid Wallace. Welcome to Oregon." He looked down at Audrey who stood with her eyes still focused on him. He winked at her to let her know she wasn't going to have to face her father alone. He took her father's hand in his as he introduced himself.

"We wanted to let you know that Audrey will be staying here in Bethany with us but you made such good time getting here, I'm afraid we have to break the news to you in person. You've made the trip for nothing, although we hope you will still stay for a visit with your daughter."

"What news?" Her father's suspicious gaze bounced between Reid and Audrey and Frank remained silent, though the way he kept his eyes on Audrey made him uneasy.

Reid put his arms around Audrey's shoulders and pulled her into his side. He tried to ignore Audrey's trembling body and continued.

"We were married just yesterday. She will be staying here and making her home with me."

"You were *what*?"

For a stout man, he had a large booming voice that startled everyone within hearing. The man reached out and grabbed Audrey's arm, twisting it as he pulled her toward him. "You better not have got married again, young lady! You knew I was coming to get you. You have completely lost your mind if you believe I will be letting you stay here!"

Reid stepped between Audrey and her father, forcing the man to drop her arm and look up at him. The man's eyes were bulging from his head and the veins on his forehead stuck out in stark contrast to his mottled skin.

"I ask you to take your hands off my wife and to watch how you speak to her. I respect that you are her father but it is my responsibility now to care for her and I will not let anyone hurt her, including you." He spoke softly but it left no doubt that he meant what he said. No one would talk to his wife that way, even if it was her father.

The older man stared up at Reid, his body shaking in anger, his hands clenched at his sides.

As the two men stared each other down, Frank walked up beside them.

"Audrey, am I really so distasteful that you would go and get yourself hitched to another man just to avoid me?" He tried to speak calmly but Reid wasn't fooled. He could see the fury in the man's eyes.

Frank cast his grimace to Reid. "I am sorry you've been dragged into this but I assure you, I have a contract that binds her to me. I'm not going to just let her run off and play house with some farmer she has childish dreams of making a cozy little home with just to spite her father."

"Well, you may think you have a contract binding her to you but, I assure you, the papers we signed yesterday say otherwise." He'd known Audrey's father wouldn't be happy about her getting married again but Reid assumed that, once he discovered the truth, he would accept it and head back to Kentucky. He was her father, after all. His love was supposed to be unconditional, flowing with understanding.

Her father didn't appear so understanding. Or that loving. He didn't see any kindness toward his daughter at all.

"Stop it! All of you, just stop! I don't belong to anyone. I'm not some...some...*cow* that you can buy and sell with papers saying you own me!" Audrey had finally found her voice.

She pushed Reid aside and stepped up to face her father. "You never gave me any say in who I would marry. You knew I loved Pete Thomsen but, to you, he was just a poor farmer who could never give you anything in trade for me. You didn't care that I wouldn't be happy married to someone else...someone else who I didn't even love!" Reid stood, shocked, listening to Audrey speak, watching her chest heave as she tried to control her anger.

"And, instead of offering your condolences for Pete's death, all you do is grab Frank here--" she flung her hand in Frank's direction, "and come racing across the country to force me to go through with a marriage I never wanted!"

Tears flowed down her cheeks and Reid desperately wanted to get her away from there. Susan and James were standing on the front step of the mercantile watching, as were other townsfolk who had happened to wander past.

"I don't want to go back to Kentucky. I don't want to live that life. In case you didn't notice, I never fit in with all of those shallow women who only wanted to find the richest husbands. All I ever wanted was my own home with a man who loved me and because of *you*, I was forced to journey across the country to try and have the life I dreamt of. And, because of *you*, Pete is dead!"

She was trembling so hard now, Reid had to grip both of her shoulders to keep her upright.

She turned and offered Reid a sad smile. "Reid Wallace offered me a home and a chance to say here with people who have treated me with more kindness than you ever did." She turned back to her father and Reid noticed she'd pulled the shawl he'd given her tighter around her shoulders as though touching it gave her strength. "And, I'm staying here. With him."

With those words, she turned on her heels and walked, her head held high, to her side of the wagon. Reid tipped his hat at the two men who were still standing there, their mouths gaping open, then walked to Audrey and offered his hand to help her up into the wagon.

Audrey settled into her seat and Reid walked to his side of the wagon, then turned to face her father. "Audrey is my wife and I intend to take very good care of her. That's a promise. And, if you change your mind about forcing her back to Kentucky, you are welcome to come out and visit." Not that he believed her father cared but he wanted to offer the man the chance to be a true father to his daughter. To, perhaps, show her some affection.

Reid clicked to the horses and the wagon pulled away from the mercantile, leaving a cloud of dust to descend upon the people standing in the street, staring at them as they departed. He glanced at Audrey, who was focusing straight ahead, her back straight and hands clasped in her lap. The only indication of emotion he could see were the tears making their way down her cheeks.

He reached over and gave her hands a gentle squeeze. She pulled her hands from his and raised them to cover her face. "Oh Reid, I am so embarrassed."

Surprise shot through him. "Why? You have nothing to feel embarrassed about."

She lifted her gaze to his and the pain in her eyes punched him square in the gut.

"What must everyone think? Susan, and James, and the others..." She hesitated for a minute, her gaze level with his. "And you." She said that last so softly, he wasn't sure if he heard her right.

"Me?" He was proud of the way she faced her father, telling him exactly what he needed to hear. "Audrey, I saw a woman who was tired of being treated like property by her father. I saw a woman stand up to a man who needed a good set down."

"But, I didn't mean to say that *you* treated me like a cow..." She buried her face in her hands again. He couldn't fight the smile that warmed his face. After everything that had happened, *that* was what she was worried about.

"I was just so tired of my dad and Frank always making decisions for me, like I wasn't even there."

He realized, now, how it must have sounded, with the three men standing in a circle arguing over who had the rights to her. He watched the road, his thoughts on what to say next.

"I'm sorry if I made you feel that way. I didn't like how they were talking about you as if you were property. I got a little carried away."

"No, Reid." She gripped his arm. "No, I never thought you were laying a claim on me like that. I was glad you stepped in to help me while I gathered my thoughts."

"Well, I would suggest we head home and forget about what happened back there. Although, I have a sneaking suspicion your father and Frank aren't just going to tuck tail between their legs and head back to Kentucky." She closed her eyes and winced.

"That's exactly what I'm afraid of." She opened her eyes and reached up to rub her temples. "I am so sorry you have been dragged into this, Reid. You shouldn't have to deal with my mess." She pulled her shawl tighter around her shoulders, something he was learning she did when she was upset.

"I will understand if you want to walk away...it isn't too late. We could have the marriage annulled." She didn't look at him, her eyes on the road ahead.

"We aren't getting the marriage annulled and I'm not walking away, Audrey. Yesterday, we spoke vows that bound us together, for better or for worse, and I am not a man who takes my vows lightly. So, even though our marriage may not be real in every sense, it is real enough that I won't leave you to deal with your father on your own."

Even as he said the words, he worried about what her father had planned. Reid just hoped he could keep his promise to her.

CHAPTER 9

A udrey gathered the eggs into her apron then turned to see where Sophia had gone. The little girl toddled over with an egg in her hand, holding it up to her. Audrey smiled.

"Well, thank you sweetheart. You sure are a big help." Audrey crouched down and let the child set the egg into her apron.

She stood and looked to where Reid was building an addition onto the barn. Over the winter months, the community members took turns traveling to each property to help fix or build anything that was needed. Audrey had never known such a close group of people in her life.

She was excited to hear that Colton would be coming to help which meant she would see Phoebe. She desperately needed to talk to her friend. And, she knew Reid's sister, Ella, was also planning to come help make meals for everyone. A day spent with other women would be much appreciated.

Sophia spotted Reid and raced across the yard to where he was piling lumber beside the barn. He heard her voice and turned to smile. He swung his arms wide to receive the child but, as always, Audrey sensed he was holding himself back.

She had no doubt he loved Sophia with every fiber of his being but he guarded himself around her. It wasn't just Sophia though, Reid held himself back from everyone. He was a kind man, his gentleness shined in his manner and how he spoke to others.

But, there was also a coldness about him she couldn't quite figure out.

He turned and looked at her, catching her staring. Her cheeks burned, the heat of embarrassment once again rushing into her face. She offered a quick wave and walked toward him.

"Sorry, I couldn't catch her." Reid set the young girl back down on the ground and Audrey ruffled her hair as she got up beside them.

"That's all right. I was just heading in for breakfast, anyway. Can I help you carry anything?" He motioned to the apron full of eggs.

"No, I can manage. We better get in and get you fed before the others show up."

They walked to the house with Sophia running

ahead as fast as her short legs could carry her, stumbling and falling twice.

They entered the house and he hung his hat on the hook, then went to the basin to wash his hands while Audrey started scrambling the eggs. The biscuits were already baking in the oven, and she had some bacon ready to fry in the pan. Within just a few minutes, the smell of cooking food filled the home.

She smiled to herself as she cooked; the scent of breakfast and Reid talking with a chattering Sophia added to the warmth of the house. She'd never experienced anything like this growing up in Kentucky.

Her house was large and her family had cooks who rushed to prepare them whatever they wanted to eat, no matter the time of day. Her mother and father never spent time sitting and talking with their children unless it was while entertaining guests.

Reid came up behind her and she jumped. He crossed his arms over his chest and leaned back against the wall by the stove. "I saw your father when I was in town this morning." She knew he'd gone in early to pick up the lumber, leaving before she had even gotten out of bed.

She lifted her gaze to his, then stopped stirring the eggs. "Did he say anything?" She couldn't keep the worry from her voice.

"He's planning on staying to talk some sense into you." He gave her a hint of a smile. "Apparently, you've always had silly romantic notions of living the life of a poor farmer's wife."

Audrey cringed. Her father couldn't understand why she despised the society life he loved so much. He never saw the meanness of the other girls, the competition to be the best, have the best, marry the best. As a girl, she was expected to be pretty and do as she was told without question and nothing else.

Pete had shown her a world that was nothing like that and she knew she'd be happier as Pete's wife than some society lady with no mind of her own.

And now, Reid likely thought she was some silly girl who had fantasies about marrying a farmer to spite her father.

"My father never understood how much I hated the finery and the insincerity of the people who pretended they were my friends. I will admit I always wanted a simpler life, away from all of that but it wasn't just something silly. At least not to me." She didn't know how to explain it without making it sound like she married him just to fulfill a childhood fantasy.

He shrugged. "I told him that no matter your reasons, you didn't want to go back home, and that you'd be staying here with me." He pushed away from the wall to lift Sophia into her chair. Audrey just stood there, stunned.

He acted like it wasn't any big deal at all!

She set their plates down, then sat across from him. She dished out some food for Sophia, then placed the little girl's plate on her special table.

"I know I need to go in and talk to him but I had secretly hoped he would just head back home and leave me alone." She was surprised he hadn't come out to the farm to confront her.

"Oh, I have no doubt he's planning something, that's why he's sticking around. I'm sure he isn't just going to walk away. Why does he care if you are married to this Franklin man, anyway?" His gaze met hers as he put another bite of eggs into his mouth.

Sighing, she sat back in her chair, letting her fork rest on her plate. "My father has a lot of debt. He spent money he didn't have in order to keep the image of a rich, society man. Marrying me into the Hillman family would give him the money he has always dreamed of having. Frank Hillman has always fancied me and has been quite insistent on us marrying. He doesn't care that I don't feel the same way."

She peered through the window at the rolling hills in the distance. "Frank and my father made the arrangement and I was expected to follow through with it. No one cared that I was already in love with

Pete Thomsen. He couldn't give my father the riches he desired."

Immediately, she felt regret about mentioning Pete to Reid, her new husband. But he didn't seem as bothered about it as she was. Reid was finished eating and was sitting back, watching her intently.

She continued. "But, that's all in the past. Now, he needs to accept that I'm happy here and I'm not going home with him."

For long, silent moments, his gaze never left her face. "Are you happy here, Audrey?" She barely heard his whisper.

"What do you mean? Of course I'm happy."

"Well, I know you're happy about staying in Bethany but do you think you can be happy *here*." He indicated the small kitchen with a wave of his arms. "Can you be happy gathering your own eggs each morning, putting wood on your fire to cook, planting your own food, then tending to it and harvesting it? Can you be happy caring for a child and her father, a man who can't give you all of the finer things you're used to?"

Her heart skipped a beat as she looked at this man, who had opened his home to her.

Sophia babbled on unaware of the exchange between the grown ups.

Before she could answer, the sound of an approaching wagon interrupted them. She wanted to assure Reid she was happy there but that would have to wait.

Reid stood and walked over to grab his hat off the hook. She stood too, turning to face him, wanting to say something, anything to him before he walked out the door. Their gazes locked and he stared so intently, her heart tripped in her chest. She was sure he wanted to tell her something, but he just put his hat on and left.

She sank into her chair. What was wrong with her? For a split second, she'd wanted to go to him, wrap her arms around him and tell him there wasn't anywhere else in the world she'd rather be than with him.

Where did that come from?

She knew she'd be happy with Reid and Sophia and was glad she'd been given the chance to stay. But, she hadn't realized it might be more than that.

She'd known Reid for a few short months, and spent less than a week living in his home, but there was something about him that drew her in. When she first met him, she thought, maybe, it was the shared pain of loss, the heartbreak of losing someone they loved.

But now, she wasn't sure that's all it was. And, she didn't know what to do about it. She'd loved Pete and never wanted to dishonor his memory.

However, she had to be honest with herself and accept that, somehow, Reid had managed to break through the pain in her heart and give her some hope for a future.

Reid was making room in her heart for a new beginning but she didn't know if he would ever let her into his.

❧❧❧

REID STORMED out to the barn, unsure of what had put him in such a bad mood.

He'd gone into town for supplies and he was surprised to see Audrey's father coming across the street to the mill. The man wasted no time telling him he wasn't going to just let his daughter stay married to a poor farmer who couldn't give her the expensive things she was accustomed to having.

He said he would fight the marriage and wouldn't rest until he figured out a way to get Audrey away from this town.

Reid knew Audrey came from a wealthy family but hadn't given it much thought. She didn't seem to miss it.

But her father had continued, saying Audrey was just a child caught up in the romantic notions of running off with the poor farm boy. And that she'd only eloped in the first place to get back at him for arranging her marriage without her consent. He said Frank Hillman could give Audrey everything her heart desired and wouldn't let her run around town in shabby dresses that were practically falling from her shoulders.

Anger filled Reid but he'd ignored the man the best he could. However, the ride home gave him time to think and then seeing Audrey standing outside the chicken coop gathering eggs in a worn old apron—it felt like a horse kicked him in the stomach.

Even though Audrey agreed to marry him to avoid going home, what if it was merely a desperate attempt to hold onto the life she'd thought she wanted with Pete? He couldn't risk Sophia or, if he was being honest, himself, getting hurt.

He knew he couldn't love her but he'd grown to enjoy her company and he wanted to make her happy. He liked having someone to care for his home and he looked forward to hot, delicious home-cooked meals every day.

But he worried that Audrey's father spoke the truth and that he'd never be able to give her everything she deserved.

What if she woke up one day and realized that Frank Hillman had more to offer than he ever could?

CHAPTER 10

Audrey sat within the soft light from the lantern counting and recounting her stitches. She was making a dress for Sophia out of some flower material she knew the little girl would love. All of the sprouting child's dresses had become too small for he, and Audrey was excited to make the dress and see it on her.

She hadn't had the time to work on Reid's shirt yet because she was waiting for a chance when he wasn't around the house. The men had almost finished working on the barn, so she knew he would go to help someone else soon, giving her the time she needed to work on it.

Since Christmas was coming, she'd decided to give the shirt to Reid and the dress to Sophia as gifts. Even though it wasn't much, she hoped they would appreciate the work she put into them.

She heard footsteps on the porch and lifted her head to smile at Reid as he walked through the door.

He stopped when he saw her, then gave a quick nod.

"Didn't expect you'd still be up." The men had worked longer than usual today, hoping to finish up. Then, he'd done the chores for the night and hadn't returned to the house until now.

"I had some sewing I wanted to do." She held up the dress for him. "I wanted to make something special for Sophia since Christmas will come before we know it."

"Looks nice. It's awful kind of you to think of Sophia, making her a pretty dress and all." She watched him shuffle his feet and dip his head as though unsure of what else to say. They hadn't spent much time alone since their wedding and most nights she was in bed long before he came back to the house.

"Well, if I'm to be her mother, it's no chore at all. I enjoy making her smile." Instantly, she regretted her choice of words. Her regret turned to nervousness, which encouraged the words to flow unchecked. "Not that I am going to replace her mother, just that I will be the one to help raise her." She was worried he'd be angry but other than a slight twitch in his cheek, he didn't make any other indication he'd even heard her.

"She will look to you as a mother, I reckon, so you can do what you need." He set his hat on the hook, then walked over and washed his hands.

She jumped from her chair, set the fabric down on it, and walked to the stove. "I had just warmed some water for tea, if you'd like to join me."

Her heart was racing, nervous about spending time in the dark of the night alone with Reid. Her trembling hands made her fumble with the kettle. But, she knew they needed to stop avoiding being alone together so she had purposefully stayed up, waiting for him.

"Here, let me help you with that. Don't want you getting burned on my account." His voice from right behind her made her jump and she spun around and slammed right into his chest.

"Oh! I'm sorry, Reid, I didn't know you were right there." Her hand flew to her throat as she stumbled backward. Before she had time to react, her other hand, in an attempt to steady herself, landed on the top of the hot stove.

She cried out and grabbed her hand by the wrist.

"Audrey, I'm so sorry! I didn't mean to startle you. Come here so I can see your hand." Reid reached out, gently took her by the arm, and turned her to face him.

He carefully lifted her hand to examine it. The furrow between his brows showed his concern.

Suddenly, the back of her hand, beneath his

touch, was burning as hot as the front. She pulled her hand away and shook it in an effort to cool it down.

"It's fine, Reid. Just a little burn. I've had worse." She tried to keep the shakiness out of her voice.

He cocked an eyebrow at her. "Audrey, just sit down and let me put some salve on it. You don't want it getting infected." He took her arm once again and led her to her chair. He picked up the fabric she'd laid there, placed it on the basket beside the chair, then motioned for her to sit. "I will get the salve out of the cabinet for your hand and then make the tea."

Audrey didn't know what to do. She'd made such a muck of their evening together, already.

She watched as he walked over and reached up to the shelf that held the medicines. He retrieved the burn salve and then turned to pour hot water into two cups. She followed him with her gaze and couldn't stop herself from noticing the way his muscles moved under his shirt. He was a tall man and from his build, he was no stranger to hard work.

Her cheeks flamed as he turned and caught her staring at him again. He surely must think she was a foolish girl; staring at a man every time he turned around.

He walked to her and set the cups down on the table between their chairs. He sat in the other chair.

"Let me see your hand."

She put her hand out for him and winced as he pulled it closer to examine. "I thought you said it wasn't bad." He glanced up at her briefly, then focused his attention on the bottle of salve. Audrey swallowed hard. She could feel the calluses of his hands as he rubbed the back of hers.

Though they'd been married for over a week, this was the closest they'd been to one another. While he was busy tending to her hand, she snuck a peek at the man who was her husband.

His chin was covered with shadow, indicating he hadn't had enough time this morning to shave. His hair was black and over long. He was in need of a haircut but she realized she didn't mind. Her eyes moved down to his shoulders where his shirt was stretched tight over his broad frame. She noticed the shirt was worn and in need of mending, so she smiled to herself, knowing she would make him a new one.

He lifted his head and her breath caught in her throat. She found herself staring right into eyes of the deepest blue she'd ever seen. Caught in his gaze, she was faintly alarmed to see his eyes darken to near black. She forced in a breath and realized he still held her hand. Neither of them moved.

"Thank you," she said, softly. Her words weren't just about him caring for her burn. She was looking into the eyes of a kind, generous man who had opened his home up to her.

She reached up and placed her good hand along the stubble of his cheek. She held it there for what seemed like hours, both of them unable to move.

"Papa!" The sound of Sophia crying out from her bed tore between them. Reid jumped back as though he'd been burned too, then quickly stood and walked to the doorway of the room he shared with Sophia.

Audrey sat shaking in her chair, watching him walk through the door.

What had she been thinking? She'd got caught up in the intimacy of the moment and let her emotions take over.

Pete.

How could she do that to him? He'd only been gone a few months and already she was drawn to another man. Surely there was something wrong with her.

What must Reid think of me right now?

She didn't want to sit around and wait to find out, so she stood, took her still steaming cup, and dumped the contents into the pail by the door. She listened to Reid comfort Sophia in his room and her heart ached. More than anything, she wanted to go in there and help Reid, to be the mother she was supposed to be for this family.

But she still didn't feel it was her place yet, and she didn't know if it ever would be. She climbed the ladder to her loft and realized she had to be very careful around that man or she might end up caring more than she should.

She owed it to Pete. She could never forget him or the dreams they had together. She needed to remember that.

❧

REID BOUNCED Sophia in his arms, wondering if he should go and ask Audrey to help but he wasn't sure if he could face her yet.

He didn't know what had gotten into him. When he came in from the barn and saw her sitting in the chair beside his, his heart jumped a little in his chest.

He knew he liked having the company but this time, something felt different. When she'd smiled up at him and then held up the dress she was making for his daughter, he couldn't stop the stirring inside him, a longing he thought was long gone.

Then, when she'd burned her hand, he realized how much he didn't like seeing her hurt.

Maybe it was the darkness of the room with just the glow from the lantern and the fire in the hearth giving light. It must have muddled his thinking.

But, when he lifted his head from her burn to glance at her face, his heart dropped right down to his stomach. He couldn't explain it but he suddenly, desperately wanted to reach out and touch her.

When she touched his cheek, the moment turned intimate and he was lost in it, but Sophia's cries brought him home again.

What would have happened if she hadn't cried out?

Placing his now sleeping daughter back into her bed, he sat down on the edge of his own bed and rested his head in his hands. He had sworn he would never care for another woman for the rest of his life. He would never do that to Eliza.

And, he would never set himself up for the pain of loss, again.

He was sure it was just the intimacy of the moment and their shared loneliness that had caught them in a spell. He knew Audrey had climbed up to the loft, having heard her footsteps soon after coming in the room. Their talk would have to wait until tomorrow.

He thrust his hands through his hair. He wished he could give Audrey what she needed. But he knew he never could.

CHAPTER 11

"So, has my brother been treating you right?
Or, is he being his usual ornery self and
making you wish you'd never set foot anywhere near
him?" Ella laughed as she looked over at Audrey
with a sparkle in her eye.

Audrey smiled. "He's not ornery at all, Ella." She
reached over and tapped her sister-in-law's shoulder
in a feigned scold.

"I do wish, though, that I could read his mind.
He doesn't say much." Audrey shrugged. "But, he's
always been kind to me, so that's more than I could
ask for."

Ella watched the road as she drove the wagon
into town.

"He wasn't always like this, you know. Reid was
probably even more easygoing than Connor, when
he was his age. But, when our pa died, it fell on him

to settle the land for our ma. Then, he had to work the land around us, too, so that all of the brothers would have land of their own when they were older." She pulled on the reins to direct the team onto the road into town.

"They all helped as best they could but then he and Colton got into a big fight over..." Ella's cheeks turned red as she flicked a quick glance at Audrey.

"It's all right, Ella. I know about the fight Colton and Reid had over Eliza."

Ella nodded. "Well, after that, Colton left for a couple years, as you know, so Reid was once again left in charge of keeping everything going. He and Eliza married and he was so excited when she announced they were having a baby." Ella smiled wistfully.

"Then, when Eliza died, part of Reid died, too. He felt guilty that Eliza died giving birth to *his* baby." Ella shrugged, then glanced back at Audrey. "Since then, he's really just kept to himself, vowing not to let go of Eliza's memory, or giving himself the chance to live again."

Audrey knew how that felt.

"But, we all agree that you are exactly what he needs. We are so glad you stayed and that you are helping him with Sophia."

Audrey smiled. "Well, I'm not sure how much help I am. I'm not really sure where I fit in yet, and I don't know what else I can do to help him."

"Just give him time, Audrey. I can see he's confused about you and that's a good thing. Since you showed up in town, he has had an eye on you, whether he knew it or not. The rest of us saw something waking in him we hadn't seen in a very long time. He just needs to figure it out on his own."

Audrey thought back to the night she'd burned her hand. She'd been so afraid to face him the next morning but he had simply acted like nothing happened. In the few days since then, it seemed like he was avoiding her.

"But Ella, I don't know if I can give him what *he* needs either. I mean, I don't even know if my father is going to accept my marriage and go home. Last I heard, he was snooping around town trying to find out information that can help him have my marriage annulled!" Audrey knew her father talked to Susan and James and they informed her of his activities in town.

"Besides, what if I can't love again?" She spoke the words quietly as though she were scared to say them out loud.

Ella looked at her with eyes as blue as Reid's. "Why couldn't you give him what he needs? Just because you loved someone once and lost them, doesn't mean you shouldn't take the chance again. If it were you who died, wouldn't you want Pete to be happy and find love again? Or, would you rather he spent the rest of his life being sad and alone?"

Audrey stared at the trees as they passed. She didn't want to spend her life sad and alone, that's why she'd agreed to marry Reid. They could keep each other company even if their companionship never deepened to love. That was enough, wasn't it?

She pulled her shawl tight against herself to combat the coolness of the day and turned to face Ella. "So, when did you get so wise in the ways of love?" She loved Ella like a sister and enjoyed teasing her like the others did. Ella was already past twenty, a spinster in the eyes of many around town but that didn't seem to bother her one bit.

The beautiful, single woman was determined not to marry unless it was for love and she'd made that clear many times.

Ella's face lit up in a smile. "I don't know anything about love, except that it shouldn't be something you push away if it's meant to be." She winked at Audrey and Audrey had to smile.

She'd been looking forward to her trip into town with Ella. But, she also knew she had to face her father today and that made her nervous. Ella was adamant that she'd go with Audrey to speak with her father but Audrey told her she could handle him on her own while Ella went to the feed mill and mercantile for supplies.

Her father and Frank insisted on staying in town and were determined to get her to change her mind. It didn't matter to them that she was married, in their minds, it was only a minor delay in their return to Kentucky.

It didn't help that someone from town mentioned it was a marriage in name only and not a true union.

She didn't know who shared that bit of personal information or who would even know about her and Reid's arrangement other than his family and the O'Hara's but she knew the information was enough for her father to think the marriage was one step away from being annulled.

She was going to inform them, once and for all, that she wasn't going home with them. She needed them gone so she could focus on building her new life with Reid.

As Ella and Audrey pulled into town, her heart began beating double time. She'd never been good at confronting her father and Frank always made her anxious.

"You may as well just drop me at the boarding house where they are staying and I will meet you at the O'Haras when I'm finished." She just wanted to get it over with.

"Remember, I'm just across at the mill, if you need me." Ella pulled the wagon to a stop in front of the boarding house and reached over and squeezed Audrey's hand.

Audrey smiled. Even though Ella was just a slip

of a thing, Audrey had no doubt the woman could hold her own in a fight with her father.

Audrey moved to climb down from the wagon but she saw Frank walking up the street toward them. He put his hand out to help her down and as soon as her hand touched his, her skin crawled.

She didn't understand it. Frank was a good-looking man, tall, with dark hair and mustache, and brown eyes. He could make any woman a fine husband. But she just didn't feel that way about him.

"Audrey. It's nice to see you. I know your father will be pleased to visit with you." He tucked her hand into the crook of his arm and led her into the dining area of the boarding house where she'd worked not long before.

"Oh my goodness, Audrey. How good it is to see you!" Dorothy Larsen raced out with her arms outstretched. They saw each other in church, and a few other times since Audrey married, but never had much time to talk.

"I will go get your father and we can share lunch together." Frank left the two ladies to find Audrey's father.

Dorothy watched him walk away, then turned back to Audrey. "That man has the personality of a gnat. Lord, I've never been around anyone so boring in my entire life."

Audrey couldn't stop the burst of laughter, especially since she'd thought the same thing many times.

Just as the laugh left her throat, her father walked into the room. "Audrey, that is no way for a lady to act!"

Humiliation shot heat into her face and she couldn't look at Dorothy.

"Mr. Harrington, it was my fault for exciting Audrey, I haven't seen her in a spell." The woman patted her on the arm, then left to get their lunch from the kitchen.

"Well young lady, I hope you've come to your senses and are here to make amends."

He motioned for her to sit at a nearby table. Frank stood beside her, moving to pull out her chair. She cringed as he pulled out the chair beside her to sit.

"No father, I've come to tell you that I'm staying. There is no sense in you and Frank hanging around Bethany any longer. I am married to Reid and I intend to make my life here now."

Her father grunted with, what she assumed, was laughter.

"Married to that farmer? You will never be happy here and, if you would grow up some, you would realize you are still living in some fantasy world, like living poor is more exciting than the life you have back home. I won't stand for it, Audrey."

"Audrey, I am prepared to look the other way

and pretend nothing has happened here. We can still be married and I will see to it that there will be no stain on your reputation in Kentucky." She blinked at Frank in surprise. Why couldn't he just accept that she didn't want to marry him?

She glared at her father's smug expression and felt like screaming. He wasn't going to listen to a word she had to say.

She caught a glimpse of Dorothy peeking out the doorway from the kitchen. It gave her a bit more confidence, knowing the woman was keeping an eye on her.

"What you both don't seem to understand is that I'm a married woman. I'm not leaving here and that's the end of it. It isn't some romantic notion I have or something I will just grow out of. This place has become my home, more of a home than I ever had back in Kentucky." She tried to keep her voice low but it grew louder the more upset she got.

"So, you both need to go home and leave me alone!" She stood to leave and her chair fell backwards, crashing to the ground. The men both stood and, before Audrey could make it to the door, her father grabbed her by the arm.

"I've heard exactly what kind of marriage you have, dear, and I assure you that, as your father, I still have legal custody of you. I have spoken with my lawyers and I will have your marriage annulled before you can even say the word!" He spat on her with every word. "That farmer husband of yours doesn't have the money to compete with me!"

Frank stood up and went to her father's side. "John, let's just be reasonable here. There's no need to threaten her. I'm sure she will come to her senses if we just talk it out." Frank patted him on the shoulder.

Audrey wanted to roll her eyes at Frank's less than heroic attempt to help.

"And, where did you get your money, father?" Audrey calmly glared at her father, anger taking hold of her. "Lord knows you didn't have any when I left with Pete which is exactly *why* you needed me to marry Frank Hillman."

She spoke as though the man in question wasn't standing right there.

"Where I get my money is no concern of yours, you ungrateful child." Her father was practically sneering at her. They stood shooting daggers at each other, neither one backing down.

"Take your hands off my wife," a deep voice growled. Audrey spun around and saw Reid prowling toward them, his eyes never leaving her father's face.

"This is the second time I've had to ask you to remove your hands from my wife since you arrived in town and I am telling you now, it better be the last."

Once beside her, he reached out and pried her

father's fingers from around her arm, then pulled her behind him.

"Why can't you get it through your head? Audrey is married now – to me – and she won't be going anywhere with either of you."

"Because she is my daughter and I will not allow it. I have a signed contract with Frank Hillman and no marriage made in haste, just to spite me, will over-rule that." Her father glared at Reid.

Reid clenched his jaw and the muscle under the arm she was holding tightened as he worked to keep his anger under control.

"The circuit judge will be in town the last Monday of the month, in just over a week. You're welcome to stick around until then to let him decide." He turned Audrey to face the door and placed his hand on her back, moving her toward it.

"Until then, I don't want to see you or Frank anywhere near my wife. Next time, I won't be so nice about it."

SHE DIDN'T EVEN GET a chance to turn back to see her father's reaction.

He kept her walking until they were standing next to the horse he'd ridden into town. He unhitched the reins from the post, then spun around to face her.

"Do you want to tell me what you were doing coming here to meet with your father? Did you honestly think he would just give up because you asked him to?" His eyes were almost black, fury boiling in his gaze.

"Well, I didn't really think..." She was shocked at his anger.

"No, Audrey, you didn't. Your father needs you to marry Frank Hillman. He isn't going to give up the fight and let you stay here just because you think you can reason with him. I can't believe you would do something so risky, coming in to town on your own to confront him!"

She understood his anger but she didn't think he was being fair. This was her fight and just because she was his wife in name didn't give him the right to make decisions for her. Including whether he thought coming to meet her father was a good idea or not.

She planted her hands on her hips and tilted her head to look up at him. "How did you know I came to town, anyway? It wasn't planned. Sophia and I went for a nice long walk to your mother's house this morning, and when we got there, Ella mentioned that she was heading to town. She asked if I wanted to go for the ride and I agreed."

She crossed her arms over her chest. "It's not like I was just going to sit around and wait for him to show up at the farm to drag me home."

Just then, Ella showed up with the wagon, glancing back and forth between the two of them. "I take it things didn't go well with your father?"

"No, Ella, they didn't." Reid glared at his sister. "And, you should have known better than to bring her here without me." Ella tilted her head and raised an eyebrow at Reid, using the exact same expression Audrey had seen him use many times.

"I figure she's a grown woman, so she can do pretty much what she likes." Ella threw Audrey a sympathetic smile. "Ready to head home?"

Before she could reply, Reid gripped Audrey around her waist and lifted her onto his horse.

"That's fine, Ella, she's coming home with me." With that, he climbed up behind Audrey and kicked the horse into a canter.

He didn't even give her a chance to argue.

[faded text from previous page visible through paper]

CHAPTER 12

R eid questioned his sanity. They were almost home now but the ride seemed like it had taken hours. What prompted him to put her up on the horse with him in the first place?

She'd sat as stiff as a board for the first few minutes before finally relaxing a bit into him. With her against him, he struggled to focus. It had been so long since he'd held a woman in his arms and, even though this was completely innocent, it was playing havoc on his mind. And body.

"I really am sorry for going in to town without telling you. I would have told you if you'd been around. I truly wasn't trying to go behind your back. I know my responsibility is to look after Sophia and I was wrong to leave her with your mother while I went into town on a lark." He could feel her body rumble as she finally spoke.

Reid would rather she yell at him or tell him he was being a big oaf. At least then, he'd have a reason to be so angry.

But, knowing she wasn't the kind of woman who would lie to him, he had a hard time staying mad.

When his mother had told him Audrey went into town to speak with her father, emotions he didn't understand rose to the surface. He was angry about her carelessness, true, but there was more to it. And, he was having a hard time figuring out what it meant.

For a moment, he feared that her father might convince her to leave with him and he didn't know why he should care so much. He wasn't in love with Audrey but there was something there he couldn't explain. She'd awakened feelings in him he didn't think he'd ever feel again and it scared him.

"It's all right. I didn't mean to holler at you back there but I guess I was worried about what your father might do." He didn't know what else to say, so when he saw the outline of his mother's house on the horizon, happiness and relief rushed through him.

He stopped the horse in front of the house and jumped down. He heard Sophia running out the door calling to him but his gaze was fixed on the woman he was reaching up for.

Her hair was in disarray around her face, wind-whipped and somehow becoming. The bonnet she had worn was hanging down behind her neck—he hadn't given her any time to put it on before throwing her on his horse. Her cheeks were flushed and when she gazed down at him, he could see she had a hard time meeting his eyes.

"I can manage to get down, Reid."

"I've no doubt you can but I'm going to help you just the same." He wasn't sure why he was so intent on arguing with her.

She clenched her teeth but with Sophia and his mother coming to greet them, she visibly fought to hold in her retort. She reached out and gripped his strong shoulders then let him lift her down.

He set her feet on the ground but he couldn't seem to let her go. He stood staring at her upturned face, her wary expression playing at his heart.

"Now, stay put. I'm headed out to work on Colton's barn and will be back to escort you and Sophia home later." With that, he let go of her waist and mounted his horse. He needed to put some distance between them because as he'd stood there, looking at the woman in his arms, he'd felt a jolt of something he wasn't ready to accept.

He kicked his horse into a gallop and prayed that distance would ease his mind.

AUDREY STOOD BACK to admire the new curtains she had just tacked above the windows. She thought they were pretty and she hoped Reid would appreciate them. She still wasn't sure how she and Reid fit together, so she wanted to do something to make the place they shared feel like home.

She knew he enjoyed her cooking; he'd told her as much every time he sat down to eat. And, not worrying about looking after Sophia seemed to have eased his mind.

But he still held himself at a distance. Since that day in town, he seemed even farther away than he had when they first married.

At least she had Sophia. She'd come to love that sweet girl with all of her heart. The thought of ever leaving her made her ill so she didn't care what her own father had in mind, she knew she couldn't let him win.

As if Sophia could read Audrey's thoughts, a tug on her sleeve brought her mind back to the moment. She glanced down and saw Sophia reaching up for her. Audrey knew it was nearing naptime, so she lifted Sophia and hugged her close.

"Are you getting tired, wee one?" She held the girl in her arms, rocking from side to side and rubbing gentle circles into the child's back. Audrey closed her eyes and softly sang a song her beloved nanny sang to her when she was little.

Sensing the child in her arms had drifted off to sleep, Audrey slowly opened her eyes to stare down at Sophia's cherub face. A noise from the doorway startled her but what surprised her the most was finding Reid standing there. Watching her. She couldn't tell what he was thinking but his rigid stance and unblinking gaze told her he was thinking *something*.

She gave him a smile and lifted her finger to her mouth to shush him, making sure he didn't wake Sophia, then walked past him to the bedroom to lay her down. She gently placed the sleeping child in her bed, then bent and kissed the girl's forehead as she pulled the blanket up to her chin.

She returned to the main room to find Reid standing with his back to her, staring out the window.

"She's sound asleep. We ran around outside for a bit this morning so I guess I played her out." The day was cold and hinted at snow so they hadn't stayed out for long.

"I wasn't expecting you home until later." She moved to the stove to add more wood so she could heat the kettle.

Long moments passed and when Reid remained silent, she turned to glance at him. He was still staring out the window.

"Reid?" She walked over to him. He shook his head as if to clear it, then turned to look at her.

"The curtains are lovely. You did a good job." He swallowed hard.

Not sure what to make of his mood, she sat in her chair and picked up her sewing while she waited for the water to boil. The dress was nearly complete and she was pleased with how it was turning out. Luckily, she hadn't started working on Reid's shirt for the day, so the blue-checkered fabric was still safely tucked away out of sight.

"I didn't hear you come into the yard. Are you done working at Colton's for the day?" She was starting to feel more comfortable around him, as the days went by, but after what happened in town, the wariness and nervous jitters were sometimes still there.

He sat in the chair beside her. They sat in silence so deep, they could hear the wind whipping around outside.

"Yes, it was getting too cold and the scent of snow is in the air, so we all figured we should head home." He leaned back in his chair, stretching his legs out and crossing them at the ankles.

"Sophia seems quite taken with you." He peered over at her and her heart skipped a beat as her gaze made contact with his.

She smiled at the mention of Sophia. "Yes, she's truly a wonderful little girl you have, Reid. You've done a good job raising her."

"Can't really take much of the credit for that,

I'm afraid. The first few months of her life, my mom or my sister stayed here to help. I didn't have much in me to give her and that's something I feel bad about every day but it couldn't be helped at the time." He stared down at his boots.

"No, I can imagine having to care for a new baby, while dealing with your grief, must have been difficult." The kettle whistled so she stood to pour them cups of tea.

She glanced out the window as she stood and saw the first few snowflakes falling.

"Reid, look, it's snowing!" With the white flakes coming down, blanketing the ground around them, it was beautiful. He stood and came to stand beside her.

"I figured it wasn't long coming. Seems like we could be in for a good storm."

Audrey turned to go to the stove but, before she could go, Reid reached out and took her hand in his.

She blinked down at their joined hands, afraid to face him.

"Thank you, Audrey, for giving my daughter a mother." The words gripped her heart, forcing her eyes up to meet his gaze. His eyes held hers and she was lost.

"I know I haven't been a very good father to her the past few months but I love her more than life. Knowing she has someone who will care for her gives me hope, something that I never thought I would feel again." The shadow in his eyes told her how difficult that was to admit.

Audrey stood frozen to the spot, the sound of the kettle bubbling in the background. She couldn't find her voice, afraid if she spoke, the moment would be gone.

The wind banged the shutters against the side of the house but she didn't hear anything but the beating of her own heart and the sounds of Reid breathing.

She hadn't regained her senses before Reid lowered his head and placed the gentlest kiss on her lips. Her mouth burned as if his kiss had set them aflame and, as he lifted his head, her free hand came up to touch where his lips had been.

Then, as sudden as it happened, he dropped her hand and moved to the stove. Her legs were heavy as iron but if she didn't sit, they wouldn't hold her much longer.

Trying to get her heartbeat back under control, she sat in her chair, her fingers still pressed against her tingling lips. The fire that his single kiss ignited within her was the hottest she'd ever felt.

What was happening to her? Surely she had felt the same with Pete. She couldn't remember. Tears welled.

Her heart ached with sadness over a love lost,

while battling with the emotions Reid was awakening in her.

She had never been so confused in her life.

CHAPTER 13

The snow continued to fall throughout the day, leaving the world outside the house cocooned in a white blanket.

Reid pushed his way through the waist-high snowbanks, pressing headlong into the wind that threatened to push him back. The wind remained steady, blowing and swirling the snow into a nearly blinding sheet, so he relied on memory to get to where he needed to go.

He threw the door to the barn open and the snow blew in around him before he could close it. Inside the building, the warmth welcomed him. The animals were moving nervously in their stalls, unsure of the noise from the loose boards banging in the wind.

He wanted to hurry with the chores so he could go back in and check on Sophia. She hadn't felt well since she finished dinner, so he helped Audrey get her ready for bed. By the time he left for the barn, Sophia was burning with fever.

He fed the animals and tended to the final chores but his thoughts found their way back to the woman in the house.

When he left in the storm for the barn, Audrey was lying in his bed, holding a crying Sophia in her arms. Audrey whispered comforting words to the girl then looked up at him with worry in her eyes. He knew what she was thinking. Pete had died from a horrible sickness and it was something he knew she feared.

The day, up to then, had been spent enjoying each other around the coziness of the warm fire. The whole while he played with his daughter, his mind had been drifting to his kiss with Audrey.

He remembered walking through the door and finding her softly singing and rocking Sophia. Something kicked him in the gut. He'd been at a loss for words, scared at the raw emotion he felt when he watched her. As he had stood examining the curtains she'd hung so carefully over the windows in his home, something made him realize just how much his life had changed.

Even though he'd sworn he had nothing left to offer a woman, something was happening, and he couldn't deny it any longer. But, even as he admitted it, his heart twisted in a knot that reminded him of the woman he swore to never forget.

Just as he was about to dump the last bucket of feed into the trough, the world around him started spinning. Had he stood too quickly? He sat on a small bale of hay propped next to the stall and rested his head on his hands.

Nausea struck him then, and he knew he needed to get back to the house.

Standing, he struggled to get to the door, pulling it open. The cold air stung his cheeks as it hit him in the face. His last thought, before the darkness consumed him, was how much he wished he could kiss Audrey again.

ॐ

REID HAD BEEN GONE for too long. She knew chores would likely take a bit longer tonight than normal but even for the storm, he'd been gone longer than he should have been. Her stomach knotted, worry about the little girl now magnified with worry for the father too, who was out in that storm.

She knew she was going to have to go out there. She peeked in on Sophia who slept on restlessly, moaning now and then as she tossed and turned to get comfortable. Audrey thought she would be all right on her own long enough for her to go find Reid.

She didn't have a jacket, so she pulled her old shawl down from the hook at the door and wrapped it tight around her shoulders. She hadn't been outside since that morning when she'd played with Sophia and as she opened the door to the freezing air, she was shocked at the amount of snow accumulation over the last few hours.

She only saw darkness. The snow fell heavy into the black of the night and she worried about how she could possibly find Reid out there.

She slowly made her way in the blackness and snow toward the barn and, as she got closer, a soft glow in the distance guided her way. She wondered at the source of the light.

She reached the open barn door and realized the light was from the lantern still hanging on a post inside. She moved to enter the building but her feet hit something solid, almost tripping her. She looked down and cried out.

Reid was slumped on the ground, laying halfway out of the barn.

"Reid! Reid, please wake up!" Her voice sounded loud in her ears but fear held her in its grip. She reached down, shaking him.

"Audrey..." His voice was weak and she barely heard him above the banging of the door against the side of the building.

"Reid, what happened?" Her voice trembled, worry stealing her calm. "Can you get up? We need to get you inside the house." She reached under his arms, knowing it would be futile to try lifting him if he couldn't stand but she tried anyway.

"Audrey, get back in the house. Just help me get in the barn." His hoarse, defeated voice scared her. She felt the heat burning through his clothes, even in the cold of the storm beating down on them.

Whatever hit Sophia had gotten her father, too.

Audrey struggled to keep herself from breaking down. She needed to stay strong to help Sophia and Reid fight whatever it was.

"I'm not leaving you out here, Reid, so either you stand up and let me help you to the house or we will be staying right here together."

"But Sophia..." His voice rasped.

"Reid. I'm not arguing with you about this. Now, stand up." He opened his eyes enough to glance at her quickly before closing them again. She choked back the sob that hit her at the dullness in the blue depths of his gaze.

He must've realized she wasn't leaving without him because he slowly struggled to a half-standing position, leaning on the doorframe as she pulled on his other arm. Looping his arm around her shoulders, she held it in place then reached her other arm to circle behind his back.

"Are you ready? Can you walk?"

He grumbled something low in his throat that she could only hope was a yes. She walked forward, taking part of his weight on her slight shoulders.

They crept back to the house, fighting against the wind threatening to keep them wrapped in the darkness. Just when she was sure her legs would collapse under her, she made out the faint glow of the lantern she left hanging in the window of the house.

"Here, Reid, you need to try taking a step up. We are at the house." She helped him onto the porch, opened the door, and then he stumbled through. She left the door open and led him straight to his bed.

As they reached the edge of the bed, he collapsed onto the blankets, no longer awake. She was glad he made it to the house before losing consciousness again; it had been sheer determination that had kept him moving through the snow as she struggled to get him to the house.

She pulled his feet up onto the bed and tugged off his boots. He'd lain in the snow so long, his clothes were soaked right through. She looked down at the face she had come to know so well and began removing his clothes. Her hands shook, she knew what she was doing wasn't proper. She may be his wife but this was crossing a line. Wasn't it?

But, she couldn't leave him lying there like that.

So, as he tossed and turned, she coaxed him to

move as she needed him to so she could get him undressed. She tried hard not to catch sight of the muscular expanse of his chest as she undid the shirt and, as she reached for his belt, she pulled a blanket over his waist to keep him covered while she tugged at the trousers hugging his hips.

Finally, after fighting to keep him on the bed as she dried him off, she covered the rest of him with the blanket and then sat on the floor with her head in her hands. The tears started to come as she faced her biggest fear - of losing more people to a sickness she couldn't control and the reality of it tore at her heart.

❧

THAT NIGHT, she snatched fitful moments of sleep in the chair outside the bedroom door. When Reid or Sophia moaned and thrashed, she'd wake to place cold cloths on their foreheads and chests. She worked furiously, patting them down with cool water and, when she could muster the strength, she'd force them to sit up and drink whatever water she could get down their throats.

They'd both brought up most of the contents of their stomach and were now retching up what seemed like every drop of water she fought to put in them.

She'd changed the bedding and scrubbed the

floors as the sickness took over them and tried to keep the room as fresh as possible.

In the few moments between caring for her patients, she sat in her chair and let the tears of exhaustion and helplessness fall. Memories of the final few hours of Pete's life surfaced to crush her further and, as she listened to the moaning from the other room, her heart broke.

She couldn't lose them too.

CHAPTER 14

"Audrey." Her name coming from his hoarse throat sounded far away and he was sure she couldn't have heard it. Before he could get the strength to call out again, she came through the doorway with a cloth in her hand.

Her hair was disheveled and her dress was wrinkled. As he looked at her through eyes pained from the brightness in the room, he saw black circles under her own eyes.

"Reid, you're awake!" Her voice gave away her relief and he was sure he saw tears in her eyes. She sat on the edge of the bed and smiled down at him while placing the cool cloth on his forehead.

"How long was I asleep?" He was having a hard time remembering and piecing together the bits of time from when he realized he was sick in the barn until now.

"It's been almost twenty-four hours." Her hand trembled as she dipped the cloth into a pail of water by the bed, then wrung it out.

She went to place the cloth back on his head but he reached up to weakly hold her arm. "Is Sophia better?" He squinted as he tried focusing on her face.

"She's fine, Reid. She was up this morning and able to eat a bit of warm bread. She's slept most of the day, too, but she's kept her food down and I have been making her drink water."

He squeezed his eyes shut as a throbbing in his head took over.

"Do you think you could drink some water?" The hopeful sound in her voice forced him to reopen his eyes. The dryness in his throat screamed for something wet.

"I might." He tried pulling himself into a sitting position, leaning on his elbows to move up toward the headboard. As he did, he noticed he was naked under the blanket.

He slowly raised his gaze to the woman pouring water into a mug. She returned to his side, bent to him, and put her arm behind his shoulders to help him sit upright. She held the cup to his lips and tilted it to his mouth.

Swallowing the cool liquid, he let his eyes close as he savored the wetness hitting his throat. He tried not to let himself think about the soft arm pressed to the skin on his back.

Opening his eyes, he found himself peering right into the worried face of the woman who clearly hadn't slept since he became sick.

He managed to gulp down a bit of water, then she pulled the cup away and helped him lay back again.

"You look like you haven't slept." He spoke quietly and the guilt he felt for making her take care of him and Sophia burned the back of his throat.

She shrugged. "I grabbed a bit of sleep in the chair through the night."

He watched her as she picked at his blanket.

"So, am I correct in assuming I didn't get myself undressed?" He almost laughed out loud at the look of horror on Audrey's face.

"Well I...I... You were all wet from the snow and I didn't want you lying there in your drenched clothes. I was very careful and I kept you covered the whole time." He laid his hand on hers.

"Audrey, it's fine. Thank you for doing what you did." He gave her a weak smile. "I just wanted to get that worried look off your face and I figured bringing that up might work."

Her look of utter shock fell and he saw tears form in her eyes. He felt bad for teasing her.

"What's wrong, Audrey? I'm all right now." The tears began to fall from her eyes and he cringed.

"Nothing's wrong, I'm sorry. It's just that I was so scared, Reid. I don't know what I would do if something happened to you or Sophia." She glanced down to where their hands touched, then placed her other hand on top.

"I was afraid I was losing everything again." She said the words so softly he wasn't sure she had even meant to say them out loud.

Before he knew what he was doing, he reached out and pulled her to him, tucking her head into his shoulder. His hand stroked the back of her head as the wetness of her tears hit his bare skin.

He thought of the strength of this small woman in his arms. Her husband died but she finished the trail to Oregon by herself. Colton once mentioned that she never had complained about the hardships they faced.

Then, she stood up to her father by marrying a stranger to help him raise a child and so she could have some control over her own fate.

And now, she had spent the last twenty-four hours worrying and fussing over him and Sophia, taking little time for herself, all while reliving the horror of losing people she cared about to sickness. He remembered bits and pieces of the night, her helping him up and telling him in no uncertain terms she wasn't leaving him in the barn, for one.

She'd led him through the snow and wind,

carrying his weight on her shoulders, to get him to safety. Then, she had spent hours tending to him and to his daughter, keeping them cool to fight the fever, and trying to make them comfortable.

She was exhausted, and she likely had no control over her emotions. He held her until she had no more tears to shed. She pulled back, wiped the tears from her eyes, and cast her gaze to the floor to avoid looking at him.

"I'm sorry. I don't know what got into me. I'm just tired." She tried to smile and he saw that her face was flushed. She tried to stand up but he didn't let go of her hand.

"Audrey, wait. Sit here with me for a minute." He didn't want to let her go just yet. He figured it was likely the effects of the past several hours but he didn't care. Holding her in his arms felt good and he just wanted to have her near.

She still wouldn't look at him but she sat back down on the edge of the bed. He heard Sophia playing in the other room, so he hoped he and Audrey could have some time alone, without interruption.

He moved her hair back from her eyes, and as he did, she finally glanced at him. Her eyes were still wet and her nose was a bit red. He fought back a smile at the picture she portrayed.

"You don't have to worry, Audrey, I'm not going

anywhere." He never considered the worry she carried; the thought of losing anyone else she cared about weighed heavily on her. Truthfully, he hadn't known she cared that much about him. Something about the realization warmed him inside.

His hand lingered on her face, moving down to caress her cheek with his thumb. He knew he was in dangerous territory and though his head screamed for him to stop before he got in too deep, his heart was softly telling him not to listen.

Having her beside him felt good and, even though he might regret it, he didn't want to let her go.

❧

THE SNOW DIDN'T STAY LONG as the next few days brought sunshine and beautiful skies. Reid and Sophia were feeling much better, after having some time to recover by spending time at home and taking it easy.

After the moment on the bed, when Reid had held her while she cried, something changed between them. The kiss they had shared before he got sick had turned Audrey's world upside down. She knew she'd never be the same again.

Reid stayed home while he recovered and they spent time together as a family. They talked about everything they could think of, getting to know each other in a way they hadn't before.

She talked about Pete and the pain she'd felt when he died and he opened up to her about how much he'd grieved for Eliza. Talking about their own personal pains seemed to help the healing process and knowing they each understood the other's pain made it that much easier.

Tomorrow, they would meet with the judge in town and finally put to rest any claims her father made about still having authority over her. She didn't want to admit it to Reid but she was worried. She wanted to believe that everything would work in her favor but, in truth, she still feared he would win and she'd be forced to leave everything she'd built in Bethany.

The thought of leaving tore at her heart.

Reid was out doing the evening chores and she was tucking Sophia into bed for the night. The girl was fighting sleep, so Audrey leaned over the bed and rubbed her back, speaking soothing words to help the little girl fall asleep.

Audrey heard the door open and turned to smile at Reid as he came in. He came over and peeked down at his daughter, who was now sleeping, then helped Audrey to her feet.

Without saying a word, he pulled her out to into the main room. He led her to the hearth and turned to face her, reaching to pick up her other hand.

"Are you worried about tomorrow?" Concern was etched into his face.

She didn't want to increase his worry, knowing he had enough to worry about himself. "No, I'm sure everything will work out." She gave him a weak smile and hoped he believed her.

He tilted his head, lifting an eyebrow. "Why don't I believe you?"

She had to smile. "All right. I might be a *little* worried."

He let go of her hands, then put his hands around her waist and pulled her in close. One of his hands came up to hold the back of her head as he held her tight. She looped her arms around his back, resting her cheek on his chest. His embrace was perfect and while guilt pulled at her, she ignored it and let herself enjoy being in his arms.

"Audrey, I'm not letting you go. Your father can try doing whatever he wants but he won't win. You are a grown woman and he has no hold over you. Our marriage is legal and binding and nothing he does will be able prove otherwise."

"But, what if the contract he has with Frank has more weight, since it was signed first? And, since he knows our marriage is in name only, he might argue that it isn't a binding marriage."

She said the last bit quietly, afraid to say it out loud. She felt him swallow and she wondered if he would reply.

"I wish I could give you more, Audrey." His words were pained and she knew that even with the relationship they had built since their wedding, and especially the past few days, he still couldn't let go of his grief. Maybe he was like her, wrestling with emotions he couldn't understand.

"But, it won't matter. I won't let your father win." He pulled back, looked down into her eyes, and took a strand of her hair between his fingers.

She took in the man in front of her. She knew he was afraid to let his heart feel again but she realized that somewhere along the way, *she* had somehow let her own heart open. With shock that shook her to the core, she realized she loved him.

"I'd better get to sleep. It will be a long day tomorrow." She had to get away from him. She needed to be alone to face the pain of realizing she loved another man. Even though it felt right in her heart, a part of her fought it, knowing it wasn't fair to Pete.

She pulled away and saw the sadness in Reid's eyes. His expression said he wanted more but his heart was closed, unwilling to feel anything for her.

She climbed the steps to her loft, curled up on her mattress, and closed her eyes.

She was in love with a man who might never love her in return. She knew he cared about her but she suddenly realized she needed more.

The love she shared with Pete was innocent and

pure, the love between two people who had grown up knowing they'd marry one day.

But, the love she felt for Reid was raw and it gripped her heart with such strength, she wasn't sure she could breathe without him.

And tomorrow, she might face with the very real possibility of facing that outcome.

CHAPTER 15

The ride to town was made mostly in silence. They dropped Sophia off at Anna's, then continued into town, both lost in their own thoughts. The day was chilly and there was still a hint of snow on the ground in places from a fresh snowfall the day before.

Audrey took in the scenery, savoring the beauty around her. The sun glistened off the snow and the sound of the wagon crunching along the path soothed her. She wanted to believe her father would let her stay but he'd never been one to give up easily.

As they pulled into town, Reid turned the wagon toward the town hall at the end of the street. It was where the circuit judge held court. Her heart in her throat, she glanced at the few people who were already gathering. Some of the cases were simple matters with people arguing over land or livestock ownership.

But all Audrey could focus on was the man walking across the street toward them. Her father wore a smug expression and she worried he already had a plan to win this case. Frank followed closely behind. As soon as he saw her, he winked in her direction, as though he had no fear of losing.

She turned and caught Reid glaring at the two men. The muscle in his jaw was clenching and he gripped the reins tightly.

Seeing how much he cared gave her strength. She wouldn't have blamed him if he'd just wiped his hands of her. He didn't need to face this battle; he had been dragged into it by offering her a home and a chance to stay in Bethany.

But, he'd already stood up to her father and now he had another battle to fight. Their gazes met and he reached into her lap to squeeze her clenched hands.

"Do you trust me?"

She nodded.

"We are going to win and after this is over, we're going to celebrate. No more worries about what will happen hanging over your head. All right?" His hands tightened around hers and his eyes searched hers.

"All right." She squeezed his hand back. She

truly believed if anyone could go up against her father and win, it was Reid.

They waited in the wagon for the judge to arrive and as she watched, more and more people started coming their way. She noticed Susan and James coming from the mercantile. Then she saw Dorothy Larsen leaving the boarding house and heading in their direction.

She even recognized old Harlan coming over from the mill. He was dressed up in his good Sunday suit and his hair was slicked back, as neat as could be.

Why were so many coming to the hall? Reid said typical court sessions included just a few people pleading cases of thievery or other small cases. Her case was a bit more exciting and, apparently, the community wanted a front row seat.

All of the people she cared about would be witness to her fight with her father today. Her heart sank.

She turned to mention her fears to Reid but he was looking up the street in the other direction. She leaned forward to see past him, spying a wagon full of people coming toward them. Colton was driving and Connor was on the seat beside him.

When the other wagon pulled up beside them, Audrey almost cried to see Phoebe, Ella, Logan and even Anna and Sophia too.

"What are you all doing here? Why didn't you

tell us you were coming into town?" Audrey was confused since they had just left Sophia there not more than an hour ago. They must've left Anna's house right behind them.

"Did you think we'd let our brother and his lovely wife face this fight without us?" Logan, usually the softest spoken of the brothers, leapt from the back of the wagon, then reached up to help the women down.

She sat there stunned but Reid just looked at her and shrugged. "That's my family for you." He hopped down, then came around to lift her from the wagon.

He set her down in front of him but left his hands on her waist for a moment. "The judge won't know what hit him when the whole Wallace clan files in." He gave her a smile then motioned to the people gathering around his family. "Not to mention the townsfolk here who refuse to let you go without an honest fight."

Tears welled in her eyes as she glanced at the gathering of friends and family.

They weren't here just for the spectacle. They were here for *her*.

She had never belonged anywhere in her life, until now. These people cared about her and were willing to support her. Whether it would help or not, she didn't know but she felt a newfound strength.

Whatever happened today, she would cherish that feeling forever.

❦

"STOP! I've asked the young lady to speak and I will hear her without any further interruption from you. John Harrington, I order you to remain quiet until I ask you to speak." The judge brought his gavel down hard as her father hollered from his chair.

Reid stood to offer his hand to Audrey, who'd risen for her turn to speak to the judge. Reid gripped her hand tightly, hoping to transfer some of his strength into her. She was trembling and he wished it was him facing down the judge instead of her.

Her father wasn't performing well and Reid hoped that worked in their favor. The man had been arrogant and loud since walking through the door. He was so sure they were all wasting their time because he was taking his daughter home with him to fulfill his contract with Frank.

The judge, however, wasn't prepared to let him win that easily.

Neither were the townspeople gathered in the hall.

The judge asked Audrey questions and whenever her father became argumentative, the judge and townsfolk were quick to tell him to be quiet.

It was clear he wasn't well-liked in Bethany.

"Now, Audrey, your father claims your marriage is in name only, making him concerned about your security if you remain in Oregon. He is afraid your husband will not treat you well or may even abandon you if it suits him. He has made his worry for you very clear." As he spoke the words, the sound of the spectators scoffing reached Reid's ears.

He fought the urge to laugh out loud. He knew Audrey was tongue tied, likely in shock at the claims of fatherly love and concern.

"Your honor, if I may speak..." Reid waited for the judge to turn to him and nod.

"And you are the lady's husband?"

"Yes, sir. My name is Reid Wallace and I am Audrey's husband." He glared at her father, giving him a stare that would have left most men cowering but the man obviously wasn't smart enough to shrink back, as he sat there, smiling smugly back at him.

"This man has no concern for Audrey, at all. He cares about one thing - his daughter marrying into the money he needs to repay his debts."

"That's a lie!" Audrey's father jumped from his chair, shouting across the room.

"Sit down and let Reid finish or I will be coming over to gag you until this case is over." James O'Hara, normally such a quiet, kind and soft-spoken man, stood behind her father, his hand on his shoulder, pushing him down into his seat.

The judge just sat, eyebrows raised, as he peered over the top of his wire-framed glasses.

Reid turned back to the judge and continued. "As I was saying, sir, this man had a marriage contract with Frank Hillman, I won't deny that. But Audrey was of age and so chose to marry her sweetheart and make the trip west to start a new life." Reid eyed Audrey, who stood beside him.

"Unfortunately, her husband died from cholera during the journey. Still, she chose to finish the trip on her own and set up her life here anyway. When her father found out she was widowed, he came out here to force her to uphold the initial contract which she'd never agreed to in the first place." He smiled at Audrey as he continued.

"She chose to marry me to help me raise my daughter and to avoid being forced into a marriage with a man she didn't want."

For the first time, Frank spoke up. "She never gave me a chance! I don't care if she's of age, her father still controls her and he and I have a deal." He turned to face Audrey. "If you would just give me a chance Audrey, you'd see I'm the man you need."

Reid wanted to punch the man square between the eyes. The man didn't know or care what Audrey needed; he only cared about what he wanted for himself. And he had decided that was Audrey.

"Quiet!" The judge, tired of the interruptions, shouted. "I don't care who has a contract with who or how things are done back east. Here in Oregon, I make judgments based on what I feel in my gut and can see right in front of my eyes."

The older man looked at Audrey. "Young lady, do you want to be married to Mr. Wallace or Mr. Hillman? If you would feel safer telling me in private, away from all of the men here who believe they can make decisions without any say from you, then let me know and I will clear the room."

Audrey's father gasped, seeing his chance of winning slipping from his grasp.

Reid met Audrey's gaze. "Sir, I made the decision, on my own, to marry Reid Wallace and I'd like to remain married to him." She focused, once again, on the judge, but Reid noticed she was wringing her hands.

"Our marriage may be in name only but I don't believe he would ever harm me or abandon me as my father fears." Reid's heart clenched at a startling realization. He didn't want their marriage to be in name only and hearing her say the words out loud was the kick he needed to admit it. He intended to remedy that particular issue as soon as she would allow.

Audrey turned and reached for Sophia, who was sitting on her grandmother's lap, in the row of chairs right behind them. Sophia squealed and threw herself into Audrey's arms.

"And, besides, I could never leave this little girl. She's become so dear to my heart." Reid knew, in that moment, that somewhere along the way, he had fallen in love with this woman. And somehow, it didn't hurt near as much as he'd imagined it would.

"Well then, looks to me like it's settled. Audrey Wallace, you are free to remain in Oregon with your husband, Reid. John Harrington and Franklin Hillman, your contract is now deemed null and void. You have no further claim on your daughter."

A shout of jubilation exploded in the hall as the judge banged the gavel.

CHAPTER 16

Audrey stood rooted to the spot as she watched the man bend down and place flowers on the ground. Her heart ached as she watched him kiss his fingers, then press them against the stone marking the site where his wife was buried.

Well, his first wife. She needed to remember she was Reid's wife now. And, the judge agreed.

They had just come home after a bit of a celebration at Anna's and she'd just laid Sophia down to bed. She wanted some fresh air, so she thought she would come out and find Reid who'd gone out to do chores. She wanted to see if they could spend some time together, alone. She needed to know where their marriage would go from here.

If she ever found the courage, she wanted to tell him she loved him.

But, standing behind the tree, watching him bow his head in grief for the woman he truly loved made her heart sink. She realized that, despite what he'd offered her, a home, a child to love, and the protection of his name, he wasn't capable of giving her more.

She swallowed hard, turned on her heels, and ran back to the house. She'd been on edge all day, experiencing feelings of worry, fear that her father would win, then happiness and fullness from the family and friends who loved her and came to support her.

Everyone seemed to love her except the one man whose love she wanted the most.

She climbed into her loft, then let loose all her emotions from that day. She needed to get herself back in control before he came in from doing his chores. Otherwise, she was apt to say or do something she might regret.

❦

REID COULDN'T STOP SMILING as he looked down at the sleeping woman before him. Much like her first night in the house, she'd lost the fight against the exhaustion of the day. She was curled up tightly and he could tell from her wet eyelashes that she had been crying.

He hoped they were happy tears.

After the hearing that morning, they had spent

141

time celebrating with the family and friends. When they arrived home, he'd planned to tell her he wanted more from their marriage. The realization that he loved her scared him but he knew he couldn't live without her. The thought that her father could have won and taken her from him had worried him more than he let on.

When they got back home, he knew he needed to go and say his good-byes to Eliza. He'd never been able to do it before because he was unable to let go of the love they had shared. His heart hurt as he sat and bowed his head, telling her he loved her and always would but that it was time for him to love again.

He sat in the quiet, coming to terms with his feelings, and he was sure he heard her voice on the breeze, telling him to be happy.

He knew, without a doubt, that his heart was now free to give Audrey all of the love she deserved. She'd been through more than any woman should ever have to endure and she had given him so much.

He was ready to tell her that night but he'd come in from the barn to find her asleep.

He hoped she could love him back but he knew she'd have to get over her own guilt about moving on from Pete. If he didn't know better, he was sure Eliza and Pete had worked together to bring he an Audrey together.

If there were ever two hearts and souls who needed one another, it was theirs.

Reaching out, he pulled her quilt up around her shoulders. They had plenty of time to tell each other how they felt. Right now, she needed her sleep. She hadn't slept a wink in the past few weeks.

He sat watching her breathe, enjoying the warmth of the fireplace and the quietness of the room. He brushed her hair back from her face and let his hand linger on the skin of her cheek.

"Pete?"

His heart lurched.

"I'm so sorry. Please, Pete, don't be mad!" He realized she was still sleeping and obviously dreaming. He felt awful for listening to such private thoughts but the sound of the other man's name on her lips was like water on a fire.

He slowly backed down the ladder and went outside to sit on the front step. He couldn't listen to her talking about Pete.

He realized he still had a long way to go to prove he could love her like her beloved Pete had. He wanted to make her fall in love with him in return.

He just hoped they could find a way.

PETE WAS STANDING in the distance and no matter how fast she ran, she couldn't reach him. *Why was he smiling? Why wouldn't he let her catch up to him?*

She knew he was mad about her falling in love with someone else and she tried to explain to him, to tell him she was sorry but she needed to keep living. She needed to be happy.

Then, a woman who looked like an older version of Sophia was standing beside Pete and Audrey felt like she'd done something wrong. She knew in her heart it was Eliza. *"I'm sorry, Eliza! I didn't mean to fall in love with Reid! I promise I will be good to him and Sophia!"* She begged them to stop walking away so she could explain.

She stopped dead. She couldn't move. But, as she watched, Pete and Eliza smiled at her, nodded their heads, then turned to walk away.

She sat up, her breath coming in gasps.

It had just been a dream!

But it felt so real.

It seemed like they were standing right there and it was as though they didn't want her to catch up, they didn't want her holding on.

With a start, she realized they were telling her it was all right to let go and they were glad she and Reid had found one other.

She knew it was just a dream but it felt like so much more.

Realizing the house was now quiet and that

she'd been sleeping for a while, she decided to wait until tomorrow to speak with Reid. She turned her lantern up and sat up to write in the journal she'd kept since leaving Missouri.

Tomorrow, she'd tell Reid she loved him and she was determined she would make him love her, too.

After writing her heart out, she lay back down. For the first time in a very long time, she went to sleep with a smile on her face.

CHAPTER 17

T he mood at breakfast was different. Audrey felt as though there was an awkwardness that hadn't been there before, even after they'd first married. Now that she'd realized how she truly felt, and was prepared to take her chances telling Reid, she was on edge. He must have noticed because he'd cock an eyebrow at her whenever she did something out of the ordinary.

Maybe she was just imagining it but he seemed to be holding himself back from her today. She remembered watching him last evening as he sat beside Eliza's grave beneath that tree.

"We are heading out to Walter Jenkins farm today to start working on his horse shelter. I'm not sure how long we will work; it will depend on the weather. It's looking like it might snow again." He peered at her from over the top of his coffee cup.

"That's fine, Reid. Sophia and I can make some bread together and we will have some fresh cookies for you when you get home." She smiled as Sophia clapped her hands, not really sure what she was so excited about. But, she must've inferred from the tone of Audrey's voice that it was going to be something fun.

He didn't seem in any hurry to leave as he sat sipping his coffee. "If you head outside today, be careful. Another one of Walter's horses was stolen yesterday while we were all in town. Found out when we were at my mother's before leaving for home last night."

"Oh no, not another one! Why are they only going after his horses?" Audrey felt terrible for the old widower who lived up the road from them. Ella worked on his farm, helping him as much as she could since his nephew was killed last year. He bred and trained horses that were much sought after by the cavalry around Oregon.

He had been dealing with horse thieves for months now. Reid said it started long before she arrived in Bethany. But no one could catch the culprit. The horse rustler waited a sufficient amount of time between thefts that everyone let their guard down enough to give him a clean getaway.

Audrey got up and cleared the table, setting some water to boil for washing up the dishes.

They made small talk a little longer while

Audrey tidied the kitchen, then Reid finally stood to leave. Audrey turned to say good-bye and was startled to find him standing right behind her.

"I'll see you later. I think it would be nice if we had a chance to talk when I get home if you'd like." He gazed down at her, then reached out, took her hand, and pulled her to him.

He lowered his head and covered her lips with his.

It was the softest kiss but her lips felt like they were on fire. She reached up and gripped his shirt collar tight in her fists, holding him in her grasp when he tried to move back.

She knew she was acting the wanton but she couldn't think straight as his lips moved on hers.

Finally, he broke their kiss then smiled down at her. "I could get very used to that."

Her cheeks flushed with warmth but she didn't know if it was from embarrassment or the kiss itself.

She realized she was still clutching his collar, so she dropped her hands.

"Don't fall asleep before I get home tonight. We have a lot to talk about." He gave her a wink, then turned to place a peck on his daughter's cheek before moving to the hook to get his jacket and hat.

He opened the door, then turned back and met her gaze. She looked into his eyes and saw such promise that she was sure she was dreaming. Before she could think about it further, he turned and walked out the door.

She knew it would be the longest day of her life as she waited for him to come home so she could finally have the chance to tell him how she felt.

Her heart did somersaults as she thought of the possible, bright future they could have together.

❧

THE DAY WAS cool as she walked out with Sophia to gather the eggs for baking. The little girl flew ahead of her, running like a horse set free. The curious toddler stopped to pick up everything of interest, turning it over in her hand to see what it was. Audrey smiled at the child's exuberance with every new discovery.

They reached the chicken pen and she turned to crouch down and reach in for the first egg. Moving along the line, she gathered all of the eggs, plenty to do some baking, with some left over for breakfast tomorrow morning.

She stood and stretched her back, placing a hand on her hip while the other gripped her apron full of the eggs.

"Well, hello there, darling. I never would've imagined you could look so stunning in a tattered old apron." Audrey spun around at the sound of Frank's voice. He stood watching her from the edge of the pen.

Her stomach dropped when she saw Sophia in his arms.

"Frank! What are you doing out here?" She saw the fear on the young girl's face and Audrey hurried out of the pen to get to Sophia. The child was pushing against Frank's chest, squirming to make him put her down.

"I don't care what that hick judge had to say. You are, and always have been, meant for me. So, I just came to take what was rightfully mine. You deserve to be dressed in the fanciest of dresses, shown off at my side."

"What are you talking about, Frank? I'm not going anywhere with you or my father." She tried not to let on how scared she was.

"There's something about me you'd have learned had you ever given me the chance to prove my devotion to you. And that is, I don't take no for an answer." With his free hand, he reached out and grabbed her arm and all of the eggs she'd gathered dropped from her apron with a chorus of loud cracks.

"Frank, let me go. You are scaring the child." By now, Sophia was crying and reaching out for Audrey. Audrey tried taking the child from him but he held her away as he dragged her to the house.

"The girl will be fine *if* you co-operate and do what I say. If not, well, I can't promise that the child won't get hurt. It's your decision."

In all of the years she'd known Frank, this was the most emotion she had ever seen from him. Normally, he had no personality, but apparently, his demeanor over the years cloaked a sinister side.

She pulled against his grip, trying to find a way to get her and Sophia away from him. He pushed her through the door of the house and told her to get a pencil and write down exactly what he told her.

Her hand shook as she searched for some paper, still unsure what Frank had planned. She frantically scanned for a way to escape. She didn't think he was very strong; he wasn't used to manual labor of any kind but it didn't take much strength to hurt Sophia. Audrey needed to be careful.

"Don't even waste your time trying to escape." With that, he reached into his inside pocket and pulled out a handgun. "I made sure I came prepared, in case your *husband* was around." He said the word with a sneer.

He was serious which meant she needed to go along with whatever he said. She had no doubt he would harm Sophia if he was pushed enough.

"Frank, just let Sophia go and I will do anything you say."

His laugh sent chills down her spine. How had she missed the true evil behind his calm façade?

"I'm not letting her go until we are well away from here. Then, we will leave her with someone who can return her to her dear papa. *If* you don't fight me. So, quit stalling and get writing. I will tell you what to say."

With tears in her eyes, she wrote the words he recited, her heart breaking with every stroke of her pencil. Reid would read the letter, believing every word, and would never know how she truly felt. He wouldn't even bother looking for her once he got Sophia back.

He would never know the truth.

❧❦❧

HE SLAMMED his hand on the table and the letter fell, crumpled, to the ground. Phoebe bent to pick it up and held it out to him but he was too angry to touch it again.

Phoebe and Colton had come with him to take Sophia home for the night so he and Audrey could be alone. He'd told them of his plan to talk with Audrey and make their marriage real, so he and she could move on with their life together.

Now, he wished he'd kept his mouth shut. It just made the humiliation and pain that much more agonizing.

"Reid, think about this for a minute. It just doesn't make sense." Colton was looking down at the letter, trying to smooth it out so he could read the words. "Why would she do this after fighting so hard to stay here?"

Reid stood up and grabbed his hat from the hook where he had hung it just a few minutes before.

"Maybe because she realized this wasn't what she wanted, just like she said in the letter, Colton." He was so angry he struggled to keep his voice steady.

"Reid, just stop and calm down a bit! If you read the letter, you'd see it doesn't sound like her at all!" Phoebe grabbed the letter from Colton and waved it in front of Reid's eyes.

"Read it again!" She sounded mad, too.

He held her stare but Phoebe didn't back down. She shoved it in his face.

Reid looked to Colton, who just shrugged. Reid wouldn't win against Phoebe. He realized that Colton had his hands full with this one.

He snatched the letter from her and sat in his chair by the window. He didn't want to read the words again. The truth was, reading them the first time ripped his heart from his chest. He wasn't eager to feel that again.

Dearest Reid,

After much reflection, I've realized I have made a terrible mistake. Now that my father and Frank are leaving to go home, it is clear to me that the only reason I did all of this was to make things difficult for my father. I wanted to punish him for not letting me have a say in his decisions.

But, now I see that he was only looking out for my best interests by matching me with a man who will treat me like a queen.

Frank can give me so much more than I could ever have here, and I'm not sure I can continue to live here without the things I'm accustomed to.

Don't worry about Sophia. I knew I couldn't leave her here on her own, but I had to leave the house when you weren't here to talk me out of going. I have taken her with me and will leave her in town with someone I trust to return her to you safely.

Thank you for letting me stay with you while I figured out what I wanted in my life.

Yours,

Audrey

The words weren't any easier to read the second time.

He sat in shock, holding the letter limply. He rested his elbows on his knees and hunched over in the chair. He crumpled the letter again, then threw it to the other side of the room.

He put his head in his now empty hands and

tried forcing his emotions under control. Worry for Sophia's safety mixed with the anger and pain he felt at Audrey's betrayal. Just a few hours ago, she had kissed him with what he'd believed was real emotion but then turned and left as soon as he was gone.

Now, he realized it must have been nothing more than a good-bye kiss, one to ease her conscience.

"Something isn't right, Reid. You know Audrey better than anyone. Just let go of your anger and think about it. None of this sounds like something she would do. Yesterday, she stood in front of a judge and said she wanted to stay with you and Sophia." Colton sat in the chair beside Reid.

"If she'd wanted to leave, why didn't she just leave with her father then?"

Reid thought about it, trying not to let his anger cloud his judgment. "Maybe she didn't want to admit it in front of everyone. Better to wait until she could sneak away without the shame."

The words didn't sound right to him but he couldn't help it. His fury was consuming him.

Just then, the sound of a horse galloping toward the house broke through the silence of the room. He jumped from his chair and raced to the door, flinging it open. If it was Audrey, she better be ready to explain everything.

A man he didn't recognize hopped down from

his horse and when he turned, Reid saw Sophia in the stranger's arms. She'd been crying and she flung her arms out for her father. He ran over and took her from the man.

"Who the hell are you and why do you have my daughter?"

CHAPTER 18

"Titus Cain?" Colton's voice registered surprise. His brother came out of the house behind him and now stood beside him staring at the man who'd just dismounted.

Reid hugged his daughter to his chest and turned to his brother. "You know this man?"

"He rode out on the wagon train with us from Missouri. He stayed in Oregon City with some of the others, while we continued on to Bethany." Colton walked over to the man.

"What are you doing in Bethany? And, better question, why did you have my niece?"

Titus threw his hands in the air in a mock surrender. "Give me a second and I'll try to explain the best I can. But, truthfully, I don't know what the hell is going on, either!"

"I finished my business in Oregon City and was

heading this way because I remembered you talking about the Willamette Valley and this little 'paradise' you couldn't say enough great things about. So, I figured I'd try my luck and head this way to see if there was any riches to be found for me here."

"Get to the part where you ended up with my daughter!" Reid wasn't in the mood for useless talk.

Titus turned to him. "So, I will assume that you're Colton's brother, Reid?"

He nodded then waited for the man to continue. Phoebe arrived to take the crying child and soothe her in her arms. She took Sophia into the house, away from the loud men.

"I was headed this direction, minding my own business, when I came upon a couple riders headed toward town. Imagine my shock when I realized one of them was none other than Pete's widow, Audrey Thomsen, from the wagon train."

"Her name's Audrey Wallace now." Reid interrupted.

Titus stared at him for a minute before continuing. "So, I stopped to say hello, but something seemed a bit off. The man did most of the talking, said him and Audrey were heading back home to be married. He said since I was headed this direction, I could drop the girl off with her father."

Titus shook his head as though he couldn't believe it. "I asked Audrey if she was all right because something just didn't seem right to me but she said she was fine. She said to tell you she was sorry."

"I didn't even know who the father was or where I was supposed to take the child, so she gave me directions and told me it was Colton's brother I had to find."

Reid swore under his breath. So, it was true. If she didn't want to be with Frank, she could've just told Titus when he met them. Reid pivoted and slammed back into the house to check on his daughter.

He crouched in front of Phoebe who held a sleeping Sophia on her lap. "Is she hurt at all?" He reached out and rubbed some dirt off his daughter's cheek.

"She's fine, Reid. I know Audrey and I know she wouldn't have let Frank hurt her." Reid stood up, refusing to look Phoebe in the eye. He wished he had the same faith in Audrey as Phoebe did.

"Listen, I can see you're as stubborn and pig-headed as your brother but I'm telling you, Audrey didn't want to be with that man." Titus had followed Colton through the door, obviously having more to say to Reid. Colton turned to glare at the man at the subtle insult he had given him.

Reid turned to Titus and shrugged. "Well, I have a letter from her saying otherwise."

Titus faced Colton. "Is he serious? He's just going to let her go and not even follow to make sure she's all right?" It was Reid's turn to glare at the man.

Colton put his hand on Reid's shoulder. "Look, Reid, I know you had just finally come to terms with your feelings for Audrey and you feel like she's betrayed you. But, you need to remember why you fell in love with her in the first place." Colton held firm as Reid tried to pull away.

"You need to think long and hard about all of this and whether this sounds like something the Audrey you love would do to you or Sophia. Stop letting your emotions blind you." Colton turned to Titus.

"Which way were they headed?"

"After they handed the girl off, they went hell bent to the southeast. I would imagine they wouldn't have gone through town the direction they were going."

Reid needed to think.

His gaze drifted up to the loft where Audrey had spent her nights and he moved to climb the ladder. He wanted to see if she'd left anything behind, any kind of clue.

He reached the loft and the breath left his body. Everything was there, her few dresses, her brush set and, as he glanced at the small table beside the bed, he saw the little wooden box Pete had given to Audrey. He picked it up and opened it.

He examined the box and, as he did so, something on the bed caught his eye. He noticed the shawl he'd given her on their wedding day, lying beside her pillow. Next to it was a worn notebook. His hands trembled as he picked it up. He knew he shouldn't read it but something in him told him to open it.

He read the last entry and the ground fell out from under him.

"I saw Reid placing flowers for Eliza tonight. My heart broke, knowing the pain he still feels for his first wife. I sometimes wonder if I will ever be able to fill the hole she left in his heart.

I was going to tell him I loved him tonight, but after seeing he's still mourning for her after all this time, I realized he would never love me like that. I couldn't bring myself to tell him how I truly feel.

I fell into a restless sleep, and I dreamed about Pete."

Reid clenched his jaw when he realized it was probably the dream he'd witnessed last night. He hadn't known she'd seen him at Eliza's grave.

"At first, I tried to call out to him to tell him I was sorry for falling in love with another man, but he wouldn't let me get close to him. Then, I saw a woman who looked like Sophia, and they both just kept smiling and nodding at me while they moved away. I was scared until I realized they were telling me it was all right to move

on, and it was time for me and Reid to find happiness together.

I woke up and had to write it down, in case I forget.

But, I now know that I'm free to love Reid. I just hope that someday he can love me back."

Reid swallowed hard. These words were truly Audrey's. He had no doubt.

The words in the letter downstairs weren't hers. And, thanks to his anger, he'd wasted valuable time, giving Frank time to get further ahead of him.

Taking the ladder two steps at a time, he moved to the door and grabbed his jacket. "I'm going after her." He didn't wait to see if anyone followed.

He didn't care.

He was going to find Audrey and he was going to make her say the words from her journal to his face. If she could look him in the eye and tell him she didn't love him, and that she wanted to be with Frank, then he would leave. He wouldn't let her go if there was even the slightest chance that she loved him.

He would follow her to the ends of the Earth to find her if he had to.

CHAPTER 19

The sun was sinking into the horizon and Audrey feared what would happen once darkness fell.

She'd spent the day in Frank's embrace, huddled before him in his saddle. He pushed the horse hard, racing to put as much distance between them and Bethany as he could. She tried to get through to him, to reason with him about how things would never work between them.

But, he wouldn't listen. As far as he was concerned, she had always belonged to him and he was simply taking what was his.

She remembered seeing Titus's familiar face coming toward them along the road. She was shocked to see him but hopeful—maybe he'd be able to help her.

Then Frank had pressed the gun to her back and

told her that if she said a word, he would make sure Reid never saw Sophia alive again.

She handed Sophia to Titus, giving him instructions to return her to Reid. He looked shocked, even asking her if she was all right. She knew she suspected something was wrong but seemed to know enough not to push it. He rode off with the crying child, promising to get her to Reid.

Her heart ached with worry for Sophia. How scared she must have been.

"Frank, please can we stop for a rest? My back is sore and I can't feel my legs." She was angry and now that Sophia wasn't there to worry about, she could think of possible ways to escape.

But, Frank must have sensed that, too.

He laughed and tightened his arms around her, then kicked the tired horse to go even faster.

"Not a chance, dear. I am going to make sure there is as much distance between us and your precious community of Bethany as I can get—just in case anyone starts suspecting something's amiss. Of course, after the beautiful letter you left your husband, I'm sure they're all glad to be rid of you by now, anyway." His breath hit her ear as he chuckled to himself.

She decided to try a different tactic.

"Frank, please, I promise I will go with you all the way to Kentucky. You've helped me see where I belong and, truthfully, I am glad to be going home. You've spared me the embarrassment of going home with my tail between my legs later on."

She hoped he would believe her. The maniacal personality she witnessed today left her unsure of anything he said or did, so she held her breath, waiting to see how he would respond.

"I'm glad to hear you have finally come to your senses, Audrey! All I ever wanted was for you to realize you belong with me, back home in Kentucky." She could feel his body relaxing and she suddenly realized just how unstable he really was. She had to be very careful around him, at least until she figured out how to get away.

Then, she would find her way back to Reid and, hopefully, he would give her a chance to explain.

Frank pulled on the reins, stopping the horse in a spot nestled among some trees. She knew no one could spot them from the road if they happened by but she didn't even know where they were, anyway.

She only knew they'd been traveling for hours and had to be far enough away from Bethany that her chances of being found by someone she knew were pretty slim.

She was on her own so she needed to figure out how to get away.

He hopped down, tying the reins to a nearby tree to let the horse have a much-needed rest. He reached up for her, and she seriously contemplated kicking him and running but she knew she wouldn't get far.

She stretched her back and legs, then walked to the horse to lead her to the creek that she could hear babbling nearby. The poor thing hadn't had anything to drink for hours and Audrey knew how thirsty *she* was, so knew the horse had to feel worse.

"What are you doing?" Frank hollered at her, coming over to grab the reins from her hands.

"I'm letting this poor animal have a drink. And, I'm getting one for myself." She pulled the reins from his hands and led the horse to the water. She leaned down and scooped a handful for herself, bringing it to her dry lips as the horse put its head down to drink.

She was so cold, the wind and chill in the air beating on her as Frank ran the horse nearly to death. The cold water stung her hands even as she reached for more.

She saw Frank do the same on the other side of the horse and as she watched him, she took note of his disheveled appearance. The Frank Hillman she'd always known never would've appeared in public without his hair perfectly coiffed and his clothes impeccably pressed.

Now, his hair was a mess, the result of riding all day, but the thing that stood out the most were his eyes.

When he turned his head to look in her direction, she noticed that his eyes, once so brown and lifeless, were now almost black. His gaze darted around, never staying focused on her, or anything else, for too long.

She was terrified. And, something that worried her even more than concern for her own safety was the underlying fear that Reid *would* come after her. She knew he would've believed the letter she left but what if he wanted to confront her? What if he let his anger force him to follow her?

Frank would kill him. The thought of witnessing that scared her to her soul.

She stood and went to sit under a tree. She leaned her head against the trunk to get some relief from the headache she developed from the constant jarring of the horse.

"I don't suppose you brought any food for us to eat?" She didn't think he'd thought past grabbing her and running, so she doubted he had remembered to bring food. She hadn't eaten anything since breakfast that morning which seemed like a lifetime ago.

She remembered the tender kiss she'd shared with Reid, full of such promise for their future, and her heart squeezed with pain.

He probably hated her now and she didn't know what her own future held. It was a long way back to Kentucky, especially with a crazed man, no food, or even any supplies at all to get them there.

"Tomorrow we will find a town where we can stop and get a bite. And, *you* will be on your best behavior. If you decide to try and escape, I promise you that your dear husband will pay with his life. I have the money and the contacts to make that happen." He calmly went about setting a blanket on the ground. She was shivering with cold but she knew he wouldn't offer it to her. Frank Hillman wouldn't dare sit on the bare ground.

The side of Frank she now witnessed finally clarified why she had never felt comfortable around him or been the least bit attracted to him.

She closed her eyes to fight against the tears. She crossed her arms in an effort to warm herself and she let herself relax enough to ease some of the soreness in her body. She sat there, huddled for warmth, fighting tears, and let herself drift off into a fitful sleep.

She wasn't sure how long she had slept but she stirred as she thought she heard the faint sound of hoof beats thundering toward them.

Audrey glanced to Frank and realized he'd heard it, too. He jumped up, rushed over to her, and grabbed her by the arm, wrenching her to standing.

"Don't you dare make a sound." She felt the gun pressed to her back.

The sound grew closer and she knew the riders were right outside the covering of trees beside the creek. She stood, barely breathing, with Frank's arms pinning her to him. The horses stopped and she heard voices.

"The tracks stop here." It was Titus's voice.

"If that's your husband, you better be ready to tell him you want to be here with me or you will watch me put a bullet in him right in front of your eyes." Frank hissed the words in her ear, then dropped his arm to hold her hand, trying to make it look like she was not being held against her will.

Swallowing hard, she prayed Reid wasn't one of the men out there.

No sooner were the words spoken in her mind, than she saw him walking around the edge of the trees, Colton and Titus right behind him. He stood in the opening in full view, looking directly at her.

"Reid Wallace, I'm surprised you'd be following your wife all this way when she has made it clear she doesn't want to be with you." Frank's voice rang loudly into the darkness settling around them.

"Well, I thought I'd like to hear her say it to me herself." Reid's eyes were locked on hers, unaware of the danger he was in.

Frank squeezed her hand and nudged her with his shoulder. "You heard him, Audrey. What did you want to tell him?"

She couldn't take her gaze from Reid. Her heart breaking, she swallowed hard, hoping he would believe her so he would ride away and not get hurt. But she also didn't want to hurt him. She loved him.

"Reid, what I said in my letter was true. I belong with Frank. He can give me all of the finer things I am used to. I would never want for anything." She tried to make herself sound like she meant it.

"Audrey, do you love Frank?" Reid stood completely still, his gaze locked on hers, while Colton and Titus kept their eyes on Frank.

Frank gave her another nudge. "I..I...do." The words came out on a whisper.

She saw the muscle in Reid's jaw start to twitch. She fought the urge to cry out, run into his arms, and tell him she loved only him, but the gun pushing into her back reminded her what was at stake.

She couldn't watch Frank kill Reid. She knew it would kill her, too.

Reid came closer and she felt the muscles in Frank's arms clench as he shoved the gun in harder.

"Reid, just stay right there. I don't love you, I never did. I love Frank and I am going back to Kentucky with him. So please, just go back home." The last words came out in a sob and she couldn't stop the tears that started running down her cheeks.

Suddenly, Frank pulled backwards, almost taking her with him. Fighting for balance, she turned just as she saw the gun move into view. She caught a glimpse of Colton standing behind Frank, holding his arm, but she realized that he was too late.

Frank had the gun pointed at Reid.

Before she could think, she pushed at Frank's arm, just as the gun discharged. Pain ripped into her shoulder as the bullet hit her, knocking her to the ground. Her head hit something hard and her world went black. The last thing she remembered was seeing the terror on Reid's face as he reached for her.

CHAPTER 20

S he felt the ache in her shoulder before she
even opened her eyes. What happened? Why
was she so sore?

Reid!

Her memory flooded back to her and her eyes
flew open as she struggled to sit up.

"Audrey, just lay still." His voice broke into her
fear as she turned her head to see Reid sitting
beside her. She sobbed as she reached her arms out
to throw them around him.

"You're not hurt!" She cried as she buried her
head in his shoulder. Her own shoulder was burning
but she couldn't let go.

He embraced her, pulling her in tight.

She heard a cough and lifted her head to see
they weren't alone. Colton shifted uncomfortably in

the doorway and Titus was leaning against the wall beside him.

Another man she didn't recognize was walking toward her.

"Mrs. Wallace, you need to lay back down so you don't cause more injury to your shoulder." The man put his hand on her other shoulder to help ease her back onto the bed.

"Who are you?" She didn't give him time to answer as she looked around the room. "And where am I?"

Reid frowned down at her. "We brought you to the doctor over in Skinner's Mudhole. We weren't far from there."

"But how...what happened?"

"Well, when you decided to step in front of the gun Frank was holding, you were hit by a bullet he meant for me." A tinge of anger crept into his voice but he took her hand in his. "Why would you do something so foolish? Colton and Titus were already behind him and had him in hand. He couldn't have hit me."

He pushed his hand through his hair as he stared down at their joined hands. "I was going to grab you to pull you away from him as they dragged him back and took his gun."

Colton moved closer to the bed. "We had him, Audrey. I thought you'd seen us behind you but I guess you were too focused on Reid."

"Where is Frank?" The men all exchanged looks and she was scared to hear the answer.

"He was crazed and fought us, Audrey. His gun went off again but, this time, he was hit." Colton glanced at Titus. "The bullet went straight into his chest."

Guilt marred their expressions.

"I know he was beyond reasoning with, so I'm sure if it came down to it, it would've been one of you or him. Thankfully, none of you were hurt." She clenched her eyes shut as a wave of pain shot through her shoulder.

"All right, it's time to let the lady get some rest. I will be at home if she needs me during the night. Mrs. Robertson owns this boarding house and she knows where to find me." With that, the doctor nodded then left.

Colton, still standing by her bed, glanced down at her and smiled. "Titus and I will leave you two alone now. I'm glad you're going to be all right. I can't believe you'd do something as foolish as taking a bullet for this old codger but who am I to judge?"

Reid just scowled at his brother as Colton slapped him on the back. "Now, we will head back and let Phoebe and the others know that everyone is safe."

Colton and Titus left but Reid's gaze never left her face.

"Audrey, if you ever do anything that foolish

again, I will lock you in the house and never let you out again, do you hear me?" His voice was gruff but the gentle swirling of his thumb on the back of her hand betrayed his true feelings.

"He was going to shoot you, Reid. I couldn't just stand there and watch." Her voice caught as she remembered the fear she'd felt when she saw the gun come out.

He stood, walked to the window, and stared out. "When I read that letter you left, I felt like my whole world crashed down around me. I was furious and my anger wouldn't let me see anything beyond the words on the paper." He turned to face her.

"I'd planned on coming home to tell you I loved you. To tell you I wanted our marriage to be more than in name only. And, that I couldn't live without you." He stood, staring at her.

"I know you saw me at Eliza's grave but if you'd given me the chance to explain, I'd have told you I was saying good-bye. I was letting her go." He crossed his arms and cast his gaze to the floor. "I will always love her, Audrey, but the love I feel for you is just as real. It scared me to admit it for a long time but now I know that I can love you without dishonoring the memory of what I had with her."

"Reid..." He put his hand up to silence her as he moved to stand beside her.

"No, let me finish. I've wanted to say these words for a long time but my pride got in the way.

When I thought you had left me..." He struggled for words.

"And then watching Frank shoot you, I thought my life was over." He sat down and pulled her hand up to his forehead as he leaned against their entwined hands.

"Reid..."

"I didn't, for a second, believe a word you said as we stood on that creek bank. I could see the pain in your eyes. I knew he was threatening you. You don't know how hard it was for me not to leap across and grab him by the throat for what he'd done to you."

"Reid, please, let me talk." He lifted his head and looked at her.

She carefully lifted her other arm to touch his cheek. She ignored the pain that shot up her shoulder, needing to feel his skin against hers.

"I never would've left you for Frank. But he had Sophia and he threatened to hurt her. I knew you'd die if anything happened to her. I planned to get her to safety then try to escape myself. He told me if you came after me, he would kill you." Her words came out in a sob.

Reid stood and moved to the other side of the bed. She watched as he carefully sat down, then pulled her over to him, cradling her head on his chest.

"I would never have let him take you from me, Audrey."

She let herself feel the strength of his chest as she listened to the pounding of his heart beneath her ear.

She had never known love as consuming as what she felt lying in this man's arms. The pain they'd both experienced in order to get together, seemed to have awakened a new emotion, a stronger love than she ever imagined possible.

"I love you, Reid." She hugged him tighter so she wouldn't have to look him in the eye. Even though he'd said it too, it was still difficult to say the words out loud to another man, for the first time.

He pushed her back and gazed down into her eyes.

"I love you too, Audrey Wallace. I am so glad you came into my life, never giving up on me and giving me a chance to feel again." He lowered his head and caught her lips under his.

He kissed her with a hunger that showed the fear he had felt over losing her. As his lips moved on hers, his hand came up and gently caressed her cheek, then slid down her neck.

Her skin tingled everywhere he touched.

Finally, lifting his head, his blue eyes searched hers. "I can't wait to wake up to your beautiful face every morning and spend the day with you by my side. If you'll have me."

She smiled up into the face of the man she loved more than life itself. "You are everything I ever dreamed of and more than I could ever deserve. I will love you with every breath I take."

His eyes darkened and he lowered his head again. His lips touched hers and she was truly alive again. She'd be happy spending the rest of her life feeling a love like his.

She wrapped her arms around him and kissed him back with pure abandon, knowing she was exactly where she was meant to be.

She was meant to be in Reid's arms, feeling his love, and knowing she'd been given a second chance to live.

EPILOGUE

A udrey sat by the warm fire watching the people around her. It was Christmas and the entire family had gathered at Anna's for the day. Susan and James had come out from town since they didn't have any family of their own. So had Walter Jenkins and even Titus Cain had joined them for the day.

The house was bursting at the seams but no one seemed to care about the lack of space.

Sophia was happily playing with a new soft doll she'd received from her father and Audrey beamed proudly as she saw how well the dress she'd made fit the girl. She had given Reid his shirt that morning and he was wearing it today. It fit him perfectly and the blue of the fabric made his eyes even brighter, especially when he looked at her.

He must've known she was thinking about him because he turned his head and smiled at her.

He rose from the chair at the table where he'd been talking with Logan and Connor and came over to sit on the stool beside her chair. "How are you doing? Is your shoulder hurting much?"

He'd been fussing and worrying over her for days since they'd returned home. Her father had been informed of what happened and Reid was furious as the man acted more concerned about what he would do for money now that Frank was dead than he was for the well-being of his own daughter.

Audrey didn't care. Her father had never shown her love but she had found that and more now in this little community of people.

"I'm fine, Reid. Everything is just perfect. I always dreamed of spending my Christmas just like this, with a loving family around, in the warmth of a cozy home. It is more than I'd ever believed possible."

"I still have another gift I wanted to give you." He retrieved his jacket from the hook. He reached into his pocket and withdrew a box wrapped in a ribbon.

He returned to her side and set the box in her hands. With the sounds of talking and laughter bouncing from the walls as they shared this moment, no one around them seemed to pay them any attention.

"What is it?" She blinked at him in confusion. He'd already given her a beautiful dress that morning that she was sure would have cost him a fortune.

"Just open it. I made it for you." He smiled as he nodded for her to open it.

She pulled off the ribbon and saw the beautifully carved wood and the words, *"Love Always"*, etched into the top. She opened it and saw the small box Pete had made for her inside.

Her hand flew to her mouth to stop the cry that escaped. She lifted her eyes to his, unable to speak.

He reached over and took one of her hands in his. "I know how much that little box meant to you and I wanted you to know that I never want you to forget Pete or what you two had. I wanted it to be safe inside something *I* made for you, with all my love." He took the box from her and peered down at it.

"I left room for you to put other things in it but I made sure there was a spot for this box, too. So, it could be put away but never forgotten."

She watched as he set it down on the hearth beside them, then looked back at her. He put his other hand back on hers.

"You're not going to cry again, are you?" He'd been giving her a hard time since they'd revealed their true feelings for one another, saying she seemed to cry with happiness every time he turned around.

"I can't help it, Reid. You are more than I could have ever dreamt of. I believe, with all of my heart, that I was meant to find you, so you could save me."

"No darling, I think you have that wrong. You are the one who saved me."

His lips met hers with a tender touch that caused her insides to melt. Before he could continue, she felt a tug on her skirt.

She looked down into the face of the little girl smiling up at them and knew she had never felt as alive as she did at that moment with her family and the man she loved by her side.

As she sat back and pulled Sophia onto her lap, she was almost sure she felt a breeze kiss her cheek. She closed her eyes and she knew.

She knew she was right where her heart was supposed to be.

TAKE A LOOK AT BOOK THREE:
ELLA'S EMBRACE

Ella has always been determined and head-strong, vowing only to marry for love. At her age, it seems like her chances of that happening have slipped away.

When she is left the title to half of a neighboring farm, she sees the opportunity to have her independence, and not become a burden to her family. The only problem is that there are stipulations, one being the fact that she has to work alongside the man who's been left the other half of that farm.

Titus Cain has his own demons to face, and taking over a farm in Oregon with a woman isn't in his plans.

To make matters worse, someone else has their eye

on the land, and they've already proven they're willing to kill whoever gets in their way to get it.

What will happen when two people are forced to join together to save a farm, and risk their lives to find who killed the man they both loved? Can a young woman live on a farm with a man who isn't her husband, without ruining her reputation, even if it is for all the right reasons?

Ella & Titus must fight together against the circumstances trying to tear them apart.

AVAILABLE APRIL 2022